Magnified

Magnified, Book One

Mell Eight

A NineStar Press Publication
www.ninestarpress.com

Magnified

ISBN: 978-1-64890-224-6
© 2021 Mell Eight
Cover Art © 2021 Natasha Snow
Published in March, 2021 by NineStar Press, New Mexico, USA.

This is a work of fiction. Names, characters, places, and incidents are either the product of the author's imagination or are used fictitiously. Any resemblance to actual persons living or dead, business establishments, events, or locales is entirely coincidental.

All rights reserved. No part of this publication may be reproduced in any material form, whether by printing, photocopying, scanning or otherwise without the written permission of the publisher. To request permission and all other inquiries, contact NineStar Press at Contact@ninestarpress.com.

Also available in Print, ISBN: 978-1-64890-225-3

CONTENT WARNING:
This book contains sexually explicit content, which may only be suitable for mature readers. Depictions of abduction/kidnapping, antisemitism, and genocide.

On her deathbed, Yani's great-grandmother reveals she has one last story from her past to tell: that of his great-uncle Yakov, who helped her survive the Nazis. It's a story of vampires and werewolves he can scarcely believe—and in the wake of his great-grandmother's death, Yani discovers the story is far from over.

The world of vampires and werewolves isn't a safe place for a human, even one with Yani's unusual family history. With danger at his door, the smart thing would be to run, but much like his great-grandmother, Yani has never been very good at running away—especially with his loved ones and the whole world at stake.

Prologue

2004

"Gramma, are you really dying?" Shira asked. She spoke around the thumb tucked in her mouth, but Great-grandma Chana still smiled down gently at the small three-year-old girl and her very chubby cheeks. Yani's sister was such a baby, but she could say things that Yani didn't dare. He was thirteen after all, and post-bar-mitzvah children knew better.

"I'm sorry to say that is finally true," Gramma replied gently. The Eastern European accent she had never lost despite her many years living in the US, softened her consonants. Yani had heard her kind voice almost every day of his life, and it hurt to know that was about to end. "It is my time, as such a time comes to us all. God writes in his book, every Rosh Hashanah and Yom Kippur, who will live and who will die. Shira, this year I asked God to take me to him. I have been on this earth for long enough."

Mell Eight

"But I'm gonna miss you, Gramma," Shira sniffled.

Mom came over then and pulled Shira into a hug. Yani wished he were still young enough to get the same treatment. He could use a hug too. Gramma had been around for forever. She was nearly a hundred years old, although since her original birth certificate had been lost, no one was exactly certain of her precise birthdate. Instead, they celebrated on the day she had finally earned enough money to buy an actual house and move the entire family out of the city.

Gramma Chana was such a constant fixture in Yani's life that he couldn't imagine what it would be like with her gone. She had held him when he was born and had attended every birthday party and Passover Seder. In fact, just ten years ago, she'd still held Thanksgiving dinner at her house. Tzimmes for Thanksgiving was weird, according to Yani's non-Jewish friends, but the sweet-potato-and-marshmallow dish was a staple for his stomach, and he couldn't understand why no one else had it too. It was one of Gramma's specialties.

Gramma had stood tall at his bar mitzvah just a few months back when she read an aliyah. Her hug after he read from the Torah while she stood next to him and watched with pride visible in every bone had been the strongest one of that day. In fact, Yani couldn't think of a single important moment when Gramma hadn't been there with a wide smile on her face.

But now she was lying in bed at a hospital, surrounded by her family. Grandpa Gideon was there, holding her hand while his younger brothers, Aharon and Shmuley, and their two much younger sisters and all their kids and grandkids hovered nearby. Great-uncle Shimon stood in the corner watching with tears in his eyes; Gramma had raised him too.

Mom was still holding Shira, standing next to Grandpa with her two older brothers. All of Yani's many cousins were across the room. In fact, the room was packed with people.

Magnified

Gramma sighed and smiled happily as she looked around the room. "Truly, I have been blessed. To have such a family. If only—" She paused on another sigh. "Yani." She beckoned toward him. "I have a story to tell you. A very important story."

Yani slowly walked closer to her bed, taking her wrinkled and scarred hand in his. She had worked hard when she first immigrated to America. Sixteen-hour days mending and sewing in a tiny basement apartment, trying to feed five people while learning to speak and read English and all of the new and strange American customs, had left their scars.

"I've already heard all of your important stories, Gramma," Yani said gently, hoping to escape from one last telling of her days as cargo with four young children in tow aboard the steam ship that had brought her and her entire family across the Atlantic Ocean to America.

"Not this one, my dear," Gramma Chana said with a very gentle smile. "This one I have not told you, but it is my most important story. It is the story I have kept close to my heart all these years; the story of survival and love in utmost adversity. In fact, everyone should listen and remember, Shimon especially," she added in a louder voice to the rest of the room. "About my younger brother, Yakov."

"Yakov? He stayed behind in Europe," Grandpa Gideon said, but Gramma just continued to smile and began telling her tale.

1944

The woods were frightening at night. They were frightening during the day too. In these times, everything was frightening. Chana knew that, but she still put on a brave face for the children. She was the oldest left in the family, and they all looked to her for guidance.

Mother and Father were smoke and ash now. Even Chana had heard the rumors about Auschwitz and Bergen-Belsen. She couldn't miss those rumors in the Ghetto, although most adults laughed that such terrible things could actually occur. Giant chimneys where the bodies of thousands of murdered Jews were immolated? Preposterous. No human being could condone such gruesome and inhumane acts. But Chana did not doubt the cruelty of the Nazis.

Just two nights prior, the Ghetto had been emptied. All of their meager belongings had been left behind while every single man, woman, and child of every age had been loaded aboard a train in cattle cars. Mother and Father had been rounded up the previous month with many of the other older adults. They had been told that there were jobs for them elsewhere. Mother had promised to write the minute she arrived in her new home, but no letter had ever come.

Bubbie had died in the Ghetto, and Zayde had buried her in the basement of the house they shared with four other families. There hadn't been a graveyard in the Ghetto. Zayde had limped aboard the train and passed away from the heat and lack of water within a few hours, but he had passed with a smile because he could finally join Bubbie in heaven.

And then the train broke down, and the lurching, crashing halt broke one of the bolts on the car door. The day was scorching hot for midautumn, and while the train idled, people died. Inside the metal train cars, the air sat heavy with human stench. Water wasn't available and the captives were suffering. The only breeze came through the tiny barred windows at the very top of the car, which didn't do anything to cool them or alleviate the human stench. In the middle of the night, some of the men managed to force the door open.

Magnified

Chana gathered what was left of her family, and they ran. People around them died as guns fired and bullets struck, but Chana managed to keep her family safe and moving.

"Mama, I'm hungry." Five-year-old Shmuley didn't understand why dinner or breakfast wasn't served. He and his young siblings always got something to eat, even when the adults went hungry for days at a time.

"We'll find something to eat soon," Chana tried to reassure not just Shmuley but all of the family. All they could do was keep walking. At some point, they would find an abandoned farm where they could hide and scrounge for food. She hoped.

"We passed a town while on the train," Yakov insisted. "If nothing else, I can steal some bread. Chana, why don't you try to get everyone to sleep while I go look?"

Yakov was still young. He was just barely eighteen, and curled in his arms was his newborn child, a child who would never know his mother. The birth had been too difficult in the Ghetto. The baby had been breech, and there hadn't been a proper midwife to turn him. Somehow, they had saved the baby, but Shira, Yakov's wife, was buried next to Grandmother and Chana's own husband. Yakov hadn't cried. Crying in the Ghetto was a useless endeavor, but then, it had been an arranged marriage insisted upon by the Ghetto elders. Life went on in the Ghetto despite the harsh conditions, and marriage was a part of life. Yakov and Shira had been the proper age, so the wedding had occurred. And now Shira was dead and Yakov had a child he couldn't take care of in his arms.

Chana took Shimon. She was starving, too, and the younger kids were going to die if they didn't eat. How could she argue with Yakov when he still had the strength to do something to save them?

Yakov continued walking while Chana guided the children in gathering piles of dead leaves to make beds. The activity distracted them from their woes for a few minutes, and sleep did the rest. Chana closed her eyes, but she didn't dare drift off. With Yakov gone, she was the only one who could stay alert to the arrival of the Nazis chasing after them. She would be their only warning if they needed to run and hide.

Yakov didn't return that night. Morning dawned and the forest slowly awakened. The birds sang and sunlight drifted serenely through the leaves. It was a lovely morning for a funeral. Shimon fussed weakly in Gideon's arms, the starved seven-year-old just barely able to hold the weight of an infant, while Chana gathered Aryeh's body to her chest with shaking fingers. He was her baby, just four years old and with so much of the future ahead of him. But the cold of the night had taken him no matter how much she begged him to wake up.

She couldn't bury him without a shovel, but she arranged his body nicely against a tree. The sunlight streamed down on his tiny, unmoving face, too thin and hollow for someone of his age. Chana slowly stood, unwilling to take her eyes off her baby, and took Shimon from Gideon to have something to steady her hands and keep her from falling back to her knees beside Aryeh. She didn't know all of the burial prayers, but the most important one she had heard too many times. Aryeh deserved to be remembered with the proper prayers, for his memory to be a blessing in G-d's eyes as much it would always be in her heart.

"*Yitgadal v'yit kadash sh'may raba.*" (Magnified and sanctified be G-d's great name.) She chanted the Mourner's Kaddish in a voice that shook and stuttered over every word. She wanted to cry. She was crying on the inside, but there wasn't enough water for her to allow actual tears to fall no matter how hard her heart had broken. Gideon gripped her skirt, and Aharon was holding Gideon's and Shmuley's hands as they all spoke their goodbyes to Aryeh. The reminder of the rest of her children around her kept her knees locked so she didn't fall back to the ground in dispair. "*O'seh shalom beem-*

romav, hoo ya'ah-seh shalom aleynu v'al kol Yisrael." (Let He who makes peace in the heavens, grant peace to all of us and to all Israel.)

The prayer was finished. Aryeh was gone, but she still had four other children to think about. They couldn't remain at a graveside while they waited for Yakov to return. If they stayed in one place, the chances of the Nazis finding them grew. Chana switched Shimon to her left arm and took Gideon's hand in her right hand and they walked on. She couldn't help one last, lingering look back at her baby, but the Ghetto had already hardened her heart to the inevitability of death, so she turned around and kept walking.

They all survived the day. Somehow. But Chana knew night was coming and that Shimon didn't have the strength to make it to another morning. Aharon might not either. Still, they gathered together piles of leaves for their bedding. Chana kissed Aharon, Gideon, and Shmuley on their foreheads, bidding them good night, and then curled up next to them with Shimon in her arms. She didn't dare sleep, but exhaustion and weakness were quick to overcome her resolve.

She woke to someone shaking her shoulder. It was better than the bullet in the head the Nazis would have provided, but she still came awake with a yell of fright.

"Chana," Yakov hissed. "It's me!" She sat up and cooed at Shimon for a few moments to quiet him before looking at Yakov. He wasn't smiling, but some of the grim heaviness that had rested on his shoulders had faded. In his hands was a loaf of bread, which he handed to Chana in exchange for Shimon. He picked up a flask and a clean-looking rag from the ground. Inside the flask was actual milk, still warm from the cow. He soaked the rag and let Shimon happily suck on it.

"Mama, eat," Aharon insisted. He showed her the half-eaten loaf of bread in his hands. She looked to see that Gideon and Shmuley each had one of their own and that there was a fifth loaf, Aryeh's, on the ground next to them.

She turned to stare incredulously at Yakov even as her hands were busy ripping pieces of bread off the loaf to stuff into her mouth.

"I've found us a place to stay," Yakov explained. "An older gentleman caught me in his kitchen, but when I explained why I was there, he offered us a parlor to stay in and food."

"Oh, Yakov," Chana gasped. "Really?"

"There's a catch," Yakov said, "but I'll explain it to you some other time."

"Yakov," Chana admonished.

Yakov smiled. It was the first smile Chana had seen any of her family wear in years. Every other happy moment had been forced and under the strain of the Ghetto. Yakov's smile held true pleasure, and his eyes had a twinkle she hadn't seen since he was very young.

"It's a catch I'm willing to pay," he insisted. "Don't worry, Chana."

So she didn't. The bread was more important at the time anyway.

2004

"So you lived happily ever after?" Shira asked, interrupting Gramma's story.

Gramma shook her head, but her smile had dimmed at the telling of her horrible tale. She had never spoken about her time during the Holocaust. Grandpa Gideon had mentioned running from the Ghetto and finding a place to stay and hide for the remainder of the war, but he didn't remember much from so long ago. Yani hadn't had any idea just what Gramma and Grandpa and all the rest of his family had gone through.

He had read about the Nazis in school. World War II was filled with so much pain, and public schools didn't want to traumatize their children with images of the devastation or horror stories about the concentration camps. Lessons were watered down to abstract thoughts about the price of blindly following orders or the tragedy of genocide. Yani hoped high-school-level history had more depth, especially after hearing Gramma's story.

Hebrew school hadn't had the resources or the time to educate Yani to the fullest extent possible. For two hours on Thursdays and Sundays, Yani had to learn everything he needed to know for his bar mitzvah. There wasn't time to really impart the whole five thousand years of Jewish history. The Holocaust had its own unit, because that was the greatest tragedy of the Jewish people, but it was mixed together with all the other tragedies: the destructions of the Temple, getting thrown out of Spain, England, Portugal, Europe, and modern radical Islamic terrorism in Israel.

Still, there was a sort of collective memory among the Jewish people. Getting thrown out of Spain had occurred in 1492, yet Yani still felt betrayal and sadness over it. The Holocaust had ended decades before his mom's birth, yet he still cried at the loss of six million of his people. There was no accurate way to describe the pain of memory the Holocaust brought to Yani's mind, no proper way to encompass the terrible feelings, but Gramma's story certainly tried.

"Not yet, Shira," Gramma replied. "I've told you the story of my happily ever after. When I met Rabbi Herzstein and fell in love?"

"Ohhh," Shira gasped. "Yeah, I remember. You got to move out of the city and aunties Miriam and Ariela were born."

"It was the happiest day of my life to move to the suburbs," Gramma agreed.

"My English was finally good enough that my teachers stopped ignoring me at school," Grandpa Gideon added. "And we didn't have to share that one mattress any longer."

Gramma was smiling again, the happy memories beating back the ghosts of the past.

"I still can't believe my Gideon managed to get into college after all that!" she agreed, referencing another story Yani had heard many times. "And then Aharon, Shmuley, and Shimon followed right after. I'm still paying off those school debts, you realize."

"I paid off my own school debts," Miriam, the retired lawyer, grumped from where she was sitting with Ariela on a couch across the room.

Grandpa Gideon opened his mouth to respond, but Shimon beat him to it.

"What happened to my father?" Shimon asked softly into the momentary silence.

Gramma's smile dimmed slightly, and Yani felt everyone in the room shift awkwardly in place. Such a dark story at a deathbed didn't seem right, Yani knew, but stopping Gramma seemed even worse.

"The rest of the story isn't so bad," Gramma sighed. "But it is strange."

"Strange?" Yani asked, unable to stop his mouth from opening.

"Oh, yes," Gramma nodded. "Very, very strange."

1944

Yakov led the way a couple more miles through the woods. They were backtracking, which made Chana nervous even though they weren't following the exact same trail. The Nazis could still be out there searching, and they were walking right to them. But the Nazis didn't appear. Instead, Yakov found an old path in the underbrush. It was clear that animals still used the trail. Yakov pointed out deer tracks to the younger children while Chana steered them away from the animal's leavings. They were going to someone's house, and Chana wouldn't have them appear smelling so horrible.

There was nothing they could do about the fact that they hadn't had proper baths in months or that they had spent the last few days running for their lives in the wilderness after hours aboard the stinking hell of the train, but Chana did what little she could.

The forest ended suddenly on a high ridge. Below, Chana could see the town and the train tracks they had involuntarily ridden over. There were people in that quiet town who had seen the cattle cars overstuffed with humans pass by. They lived in their quaint houses with their happy families, went to their churches and community centers, and ignored the human suffering that must pass by on the train tracks multiple times every week. There were even houses right next to the tracks; the occupants could not have missed their cries for help, for food and water, for fresh air.

Yet the train had gone by, and no one had done anything to save them.

Chana almost understood why. If she and her family had suffered so much at the hands of the Nazis just because they were Jewish, how would a stranger fare when caught helping a Jew? Probably worse, Chana guessed. Still, purposeful ignorance was deplorable. She turned her back on the town and followed Yakov along the ridge.

There was a gigantic manor outside the town. They had to sneak down the steep slope of the ridge and along backstreets and alleys on the outskirts of town to get to the gated entrance of the long driveway. Yakov pulled out a key from inside his shirt and unlocked the gate. Chana ushered everyone through and waited while Yakov relocked the gate and tucked the key away again.

The driveway was extensive. The longest part of the journey shouldn't be a simple driveway; the distance was nothing compared to how far they had run after the train breakdown, but that was how still how these few feet of road felt. Her fear and anticipation of what they would find at the end of the drive held Chana in check, but eventually the full glory of the manor came into view.

From what she could see from the driveway, the building had at least three floors and two full wings. It was old, hand-built from stone mined centuries ago. Ivy grew along one wall, and the gardens looked untended.

Yakov didn't bother to knock. The front door was unlocked and led into a darkened foyer. Heavy drapes were pulled across the grand windows, and white sheets covered the chandelier and furniture. Chana couldn't honestly see much of the house as they were led along carpeted floors on the first floor until they reached the back of the building. Yakov again didn't knock as he pushed open a door to a large parlor.

Three long couches covered in sheets were set to one side and an armchair almost as large as a couch was situated next to the empty fireplace.

"You can stay here," Yakov explained. "I'll go get some wood to start a fire."

Magnified

He left. Chana stepped tentatively into the room, but Gideon and Aharon didn't wait. They pulled Shmuley in with them and began exploring. Sheets were pulled from furniture, and only Chana's reprimand kept them from being tossed on the floor. She would have to properly fold them later.

"Mama, look at this," Gideon said, awe in his voice. He was standing next to an open doorway across the room and pointing inside. Chana joined him and gasped. It was a bathroom with a porcelain sink, tub, and toilet. She hadn't expected such modern conveniences in such an old house. Tentatively, she reached out and twisted the handle on the sink. Clear, icy-cold water gushed out, flowing quickly through the pipes without a hint of rust or blockage. She shut the cold tap off and turned on the hot, but hot water was too much to hope for.

"It's drinkable," Yakov called from behind her. "The boiler is broken, but there's a big enough kettle that you can heat over the fire." Chana heard the crackle of flames and turned around to see Yakov outlined sharply by the fire as the damp kindling caught and the wood began to smoke. He looked light, as if something good had overtaken the hell they had experienced over the last years. Yet there was still a touch of darkness in his face that she couldn't place. She only saw it thanks to the light from the fire, and as soon as Yakov stood, it vanished from sight.

She would have to sit down and speak with Yakov soon, but there were other priorities that should be taken care of first. She picked up the heavy kettle and filled it with water from the tub. It hung neatly on a hook over the fire to heat while she filled the tub with cold water and roughly stripped all three of her children. Their clothes made a stinking pile in the corner of the bathroom—another long-needed task she would get to remedy soon.

The fire was hot so it didn't take too long for the water to heat. She used the folds of her skirt to protect her hand as she lugged the kettle into the bathroom and then poured the hot water into the cold bath until it was nice and warm.

Yakov took the kettle from her when she was done and passed over an entire bar of fresh soap. Chana couldn't believe it. She hadn't seen real soap since before her family had been forced from their home and relocated to the Ghetto. She stared at it for a very long moment while Yakov smiled and her children shivered in their nakedness. Shmuley began to inch his way out of the bathroom, as if he could escape the inevitable bath, but Yakov pressed the soap into her hands and the matter was decided.

Gideon, Aharon, and Shmuley were scrubbed within an inch of their lives and then sent to dry in front of the fire. Shimon was next, held carefully above the water as he got his first hot bath ever, and then was passed to Gideon to mind while she ruthlessly scrubbed their clothes. Children and clothing were laid out by the fire to dry while Chana took her own bath. She emerged, feeling human again, and put on her still-wet shift. The water was black by the time she finished with it, and Chana was glad to pull the drain plug and let the water vanish.

Shimon was dressed in clothes that weren't his, Chana realized when she located the baby tucked deep into the armchair where he wouldn't roll. Smallclothes had also been found for her boys, and a new set was laid out for her as well.

"Uncle Yakov brought them," Gideon said in explanation. Chana changed clothes and joined her family by the fire, where bread and smoked meat had been left as well.

Where was this bounty coming from? Chana worried about the price Yakov was paying for clothes, food, and shelter. Plus, luxuries like soap were beyond anything Chana had ever imagined. She couldn't begin to repay such kindness, yet Yakov had taken it upon himself. She would find some way to help Yakov, some way to express her gratitude to their benefactor.

The meat probably wasn't kosher, but food was food, and Chana made sure everyone ate. The baby had more fresh milk, heavy with cream, and then drifted off to sleep. Everyone got a soft couch to sleep on, and Chana fell asleep feeling safe for the first time in years.

Winter came, and the world outside their windows grew white and cold. Every day Yakov brought them more wood from the woodpile outside. Once a week, he would journey to town to purchase fresh goods for them to eat, although Chana couldn't guess where he had gotten the money to do so. He had shown her where the kitchen was so she could prepare meals for the family with whatever he brought back.

The children spent their days recovering. It was a slow process, but one of Chana's happiest days was when all three of her remaining children were strong enough to go outside and run around. They could act like children again! There was a gaping hole where Aryeh had once been, and as her children ran around, Chana finally found the strength to cry and to mourn for her lost baby. Just one more day of life and Aryeh could have been running around with his brothers, but no one knew what the future held, and God had taken Aryeh to peace and sanctuary early.

Safety and good meals had brought them all back from the brink of death, even if they still had to remain quiet while playing for fear that the people in the town might overhear and report them to the Nazis. Even Chana had gotten involved with a snow fight on a couple of memorable occasions.

It was an almost undisturbed time, free of most worry or strife. But Chana still worried. She didn't know what was happening in the outside world. Had the Nazis taken control of all of Europe? When would they descend on the town below and discover the Jews hidden within the manor? The ferocity of the Nazis woke her from nightmares at night, and she worried that the war would be lost and Nazism would spread into their simple world again.

Chana had no doubt that the first place the Nazis would visit when they came to this town was this manor, which had plenty of opulence for them to steal. There wasn't a train station in the town; maybe that was why they hadn't already taken it over. Regardless, Chana prepared to run out the back door into the woods as the Nazis smashed in through the front.

Most of all, she worried about Yakov. He spent time with the family. He would run around outside with them during the day and feed his son in the evenings. He made sure they had everything they needed. But he didn't sleep with them at night, and there were entire days when he didn't appear at all.

Chana had caught him whistling a happy tune once, when she had been walking to the kitchen to make lunch. There was always a smile on his face, but some days he also looked pale and ill. He was happy, that much she could tell, which was why she didn't confront him about his strange behavior.

In the dead of winter, Yakov caught a cold. He had gotten wet during a snow battle with the children and hadn't dried off completely before heading back outside to gather more wood. Within a day, the sniffles turned into a full-blown fever and cough.

Chana lugged extra wood inside by herself, and from the food supplies on hand, she put together a rough chicken soup for dinner. Yakov ate what he could, but the children enjoyed it much more than he did. For the first time, Yakov slept in the room with them. He curled up on the armchair with Shimon, but Chana quickly took the baby so he wouldn't catch Yakov's bug.

For two more nights, Yakov coughed and shivered in front of the fire. As the third night approached, Yakov sat with Chana on her couch.

"I need you to do me a huge favor," Yakov rasped, his voice gone from all the coughing.

"What do you need?" Chana asked immediately. Yakov hadn't been subtle. He was sick, yes, but Chana hadn't missed the longing looks at the door or the whimpering dreams that left him stumbling in embarrassment into the bathroom. Someone was absent from Yakov's life, someone of a sexual nature, and whom Yakov was visibly missing. Chana might be female, but there were some things about a man—even if the man was her brother—that she couldn't miss. A man in love and missing his partner was impossible to overlook.

"There is a man living here. I'm supposed to meet with him every Wednesday night, but I've been spending most nights there as well." He was blushing despite the fever, Chana realized. It was hard for him to tell her this, but then he didn't realize what she had surmised. She might have been happily married and very pregnant with Aharon and then Shmuley a year later, but even she had noticed the glances Yakov had been sending after other young men in the past. Women had never interested Yakov. Their mother had despaired of him ever finding a wife and had been one of the loudest advocates in the Ghetto for his arranged marriage to Shira. That he had managed to have a child with Shira was surprising, but he loved Shimon as any father did.

She smiled at Yakov, understanding at last what the relationship was between her brother and their benefactor. She hoped he wasn't selling his body in return for their care, but at the very least she could ensure that Yakov was being treated well. Chana got directions to a basement room, of all places, and once the children were asleep she headed downstairs.

The house really was huge, and the basement was a maze. Chana made sure to follow Yakov's directions exactly out of fear she would get lost. The hallways were dark and built from identical gray stone. She was carrying a lit candle as she counted off left and right turns, because that was the only way to see anything. Finally, the hallway she was walking down ended in a heavy wooden door. She knocked and waited.

"Enter," a voice called. It was definitely male, but she couldn't tell anything else about the man Yakov was so enamored with.

The door was heavy, and it took some effort for her to push it open. The room beyond was pitch black. Her candle barely lit the area just around her; she couldn't see anything else at all.

"Where is Yakov?" the voice asked. Chana looked to her right, where she thought the voice was coming from. Even lifting the candle higher couldn't penetrate the dark.

"My brother is sick. He has a cold and doesn't want to pass it on to you. He sent me down here to tell you he isn't avoiding you on purpose."

"I had hoped not," the voice mused. "But one cannot simply assume. So you are his sister, Chana. He speaks of you often."

"Yakov just told me about you today," Chana admitted politely, "but I could tell these past few days that he was missing someone."

"That is gratifying to hear. I find that I have been missing him as well. Come closer, Chana. Let us speak of something else for a moment."

Chana did as she was asked, hoping she didn't trip over something she couldn't see in the dark. Eventually, she made out a large chair and the vague outline of a man sitting in that chair. He was a tall man; she discerned that much.

After a few more steps, she started to make out his features. High cheekbones, full lips, and a pert nose. She would have swooned a little herself had she been interested in looking for love. Her husband was too recently passed, the wound too new, for Yakov's stranger to do more than make her catch her breath. For Yakov, the man must have been irresistible.

"I must confess I have grown used to the comfort having Yakov with me provides. He is a truly interesting person and I enjoy his company, but he has been giving me something more that I find I need very much at the moment."

Chana almost took a step backward. There was something in his voice that she didn't like. She wasn't afraid, but she certainly wasn't happy with what his tone portended.

"No need to be afraid, Chana. I simply require your hand."

She offered her left hand, the one not holding the candle, and he unfolded from the chair and gently took her hand in his.

His eyes were blue, she noticed absentmindedly. Her worries had vanished. She watched almost in a daze as the man turned her hand palm up and lifted her wrist to his mouth. There were fangs there, Chana saw, and they pierced her wrist with deceptive ease. He started to suck, and Chana felt her eyes slide closed.

Someone was skulking in the kitchen. Martin could feel the strange heartbeat. It wouldn't do for the villagers to get uppity. He wouldn't condone thieves. Clearly, something would have to be done to halt the invader, and Martin was the only one in the house who could do so. Martin found his feet and began the journey upstairs, moving at a jog so he could catch the intruder before he tried to leave.

Martin stepped into the kitchen on silent feet and made his way over to the pantry where the heart was frantically beating. The door pulled open on well-oiled hinges, and inside Martin found a young man piling the loaves of bread Martin kept in the house for the sake of appearances into a dirty shirt.

"You are not the thief I expected to see," Martin said softly. The young man jumped and spun around. Martin had meant to say more, perhaps to yell and frighten off the invader, but his mouth snapped shut instead. The brown hair was overgrown and roughly cut, as if a dull knife had been used in a futile attempt to tame the curls. His eyes caught Martin's attention most. Wide with fear and soft brown, they were overemphasized by cheekbones sunken with hunger, but somehow they tugged on a part of Martin that hadn't felt alive in at least a century.

Those eyes widened even more as they took in Martin standing aggressively over him. Martin didn't sense fear. In fact, he thought he might smell lust. How…invigorating.

Martin certainly felt something for the thief, and he knew the thief was feeling something in return. Perhaps he would see if this shared lust would blossom. It might be interesting, and perhaps the thief might be the evasive forever companion Martin had despaired of ever finding. Yes, it was certainly worth a try.

Chana blinked and refocused. Martin was sitting in his chair again, and her wrist was back at her side and unblemished. Still, she knew what had happened. Her blood had been taken while she had been forcibly kept from protesting. Martin wasn't human. She didn't know what to call him, but "human" was out.

She took a quick, involuntary step back, looking uncomprehendingly at her wrist, and then up at Martin. She was scared, yet at the same time she knew what cruelty and evil really was like from her time with the Nazis. Martin wasn't human and that fact frightened her, but he also wasn't evil. Chana didn't step forward again—she couldn't make herself go that far—but she did stiffen her knees and her back to show Martin she wasn't afraid of him.

Yakov was selling his blood in return for their safety, and Martin could be giving them a place to stay only to ensure he had a fresh supply. It would be so easy for Martin to kill them all to ensure their silence if Chana tried to run for help. Yet, that thought didn't quite fit with the way Yakov had been behaving lately. The smiles and happy whistling hadn't been caused by just anyone.

"You won't hurt Yakov," she said firmly, trying to keep her voice from shaking. If Yakov was happy with Martin, then she really couldn't stop him from spending time with Martin, no matter what Martin was. Yakov had been so unhappy in the Ghetto, forced to hide his sexual preferences to the point of agreeing to an arranged marriage and having a child. Martin could finally give Yakov what he had been missing. From what Chana could tell, Yakov was more than happy. Of course, she could be wrong, but for some reason she didn't think so.

"No," Martin replied after a long moment of studying her. "No, I will not harm Yakov. As I said, I have found that I care for him much more than any other human I have dallied with. Should he agree, I would like to keep him with me for a very long time. Now, I will go collect him from your parlor and keep him with me until his fever is reduced. If I give him some of my blood, he should recover swiftly."

Chana's immediate reaction was to open her mouth and deny Martin's claim, but he abruptly stood from his chair, and she snapped her mouth shut with the words unspoken. What if Martin's power was with blood? That would explain why he had needed to take some from her. She should be grateful that he could heal Yakov's terrible cold. It was Yakov's decision anyway, Chana realized. He was the one who had chosen to be with Martin, and even with the cold, he was coherent enough to make his own decisions. The idea of taking Martin's blood disgusted Chana, but then she was afraid of Martin whereas Yakov was not.

Martin led the way out of his room and back out into the maze of hallways. He walked slowly so Chana could keep up, but let her lead the way into the parlor in case any of the children had woken. She didn't want the sudden appearance of a stranger to scare them. Only Yakov was still awake, and he wobbled tiredly to his feet when Martin followed Chana inside.

"Martin," Yakov gasped. "Are you all right?"

"I feel I should be the one asking such a question," Martin replied. He had moved too quickly for Chana to follow with her eyes. Suddenly, he was gently holding Yakov's arms and pulling Yakov to his chest. "Your fever is quite high, Yakov. You should not have hidden this from me."

"I didn't want you to get sick!" Yakov insisted. "If you drank from me and caught my cold..." he trailed off ominously.

Martin laughed. "Vampire blood kills all pathogens. My dear Yakov, I can heal you from this quite easily." He made to guide Yakov from the room, but Yakov put out a hand to stop him.

"I'm sorry, Chana. I should have told you everything before I let you go downstairs," he said contritely.

Magnified

Chana grumbled to herself, but she kept her voice soft because of the children. "Yes, you should have. That was certainly quite the fright, and I don't appreciate it. He had better take care of you for as long as he claims he can, or he'll have me to hear from." Her words were the ones in her heart, not her head. It was Yakov's choice, she had to remind herself yet again. Yakov had suffered enough in the Ghetto. He deserved this happiness, even if she didn't understand it and was still scared of what Martin was.

"Thank you, Chana," Yakov breathed.

"I won't even tell Mother's grave that you're joining with a goy," she added snidely, but with a small smile on her face.

Yakov let out an involuntary laugh. "No, don't do that. She'll haunt me with guilt for the next hundred years."

"Goy?" Martin asked as he finally led Yakov away.

"Non-Jew," she heard Yakov explain in the hall. "It's probably making Mother and Father spin in their graves, wherever they happen to be buried." If their bodies were buried at all.

Chana closed the door behind them and returned to her couch and her children. Shimon was Yakov's by birth, but she had the feeling that he would be her child while he was growing up. Yakov wasn't going to leave Martin, but he couldn't raise the baby on his own while Chana went wherever it was safe to go once the war was over. He wouldn't know how. Women raised the children while the men worked and studied Torah; it wasn't right to leave Yakov in charge of a child. No, she would be bringing Shimon with her as her own fifth son. It would be better for Yakov and for Shimon in the long run.

As long as Yakov was happy, she couldn't begrudge him the extra work.

1945

Winter was coming to a close when the army marched into the city below the manor. Gideon noticed the commotion first. He had scrambled to the third floor and snuck a peek out of a high window before returning to report his findings.

"They're not flying Nazi flags," he insisted. "They're red-and-white striped with a blue patch in one corner."

Yakov had gone to investigate and returned with a soldier in tow.

"He's American," Yakov said at the door to the parlor when Chana met them both with her fists held high and her teeth barred in fighting fright. There was no way she was getting on another cattle car to be driven to her death with her children. "And he's Jewish. Can you believe it? They allow Jews to be soldiers!"

"They let Jews be soldiers in Germany during the Great War," Chana had replied stiffly, but she eventually relented and let the soldier into their parlor.

"My name is Daniel," he said in a poor mix of Hebrew and Yiddish. Those were the only languages they had in common, apparently, but neither of those languages were a strength for Daniel. "We have won the war and are traveling through Poland to ensure there are no more Nazi militias hiding in the woods. We have seen horrors." He spoke tentatively about the Kraków-Płaszów concentration camp his soldiers had liberated, conscious of the small children nearby and Chana's dawning horror of just what they had escaped. "You can come with us. We will find you a place to go. Many Jews have traveled back home, but just as many are going to Palestine or America."

Magnified

Chana slowly sat down on a couch and stared helplessly at the soldier. The war was over. It was all over. The pain, the death, the sorrow, was all over. She couldn't believe it. They had lived in fear for so long that the idea that she and her family were really and truly safe was almost beyond her.

Then the implications started to unfold. She couldn't return home. Chana doubted there was a home to return to, and if there were, it would never be her home again. Homes were supposed to be places of safety and warmth, not filled with remembrances of being pulled from her bed in the middle of the night and forced onto a train to take her to the Ghetto. No, her home would be filled with the ghosts of everyone she had lost. Her grandparents, parents, siblings, husband, and Aryeh. There were aunts and uncles, cousins, too, whom she had never heard from again, but whose memories would be infused in the very bricks.

Still, she ought to say goodbye and see if there was anything salvageable from their old life. They couldn't travel to America with just the clothes on their backs. So that decision was made. They would go home and take back what was left. Then they would head to the port.

Yakov wouldn't be joining them, she realized moments before she opened her mouth to answer the soldier. She glanced over at Yakov and saw his unhappy frown.

"I will travel with you to the port," he insisted when he caught her looking at him. "I can be away for that long, and he would want me to make certain you started your journey in safety."

The next morning, Chana, Gideon, Aharon, Shmuley, Shimon, and Yakov joined the soldiers in the town. Yakov looked exhausted, but Chana didn't point that out. She wouldn't be surprised if he had spent the entire night awake in order to spend as much time as possible with Martin. A passenger train arrived in the town, one with real seats and baggage storage. The American soldier made sure her family was situated and that they also had their tickets to the port tucked safely away. The paperwork for their visas would be waiting for them in the port offices, sent ahead via messenger. Chana tried not to think about how much of Martin's money had been used to so quickly arrange their passage.

The train ride was silent. Chana looked out the window as the countryside whizzed by and couldn't help thinking that she was backtracking. They would pass through the Ghetto station where they had been loaded onto cattle cars; they would travel down the tracks that had led them to the Ghetto in the first place; and they would arrive in a few more hours at the place Chana had once called home. She fought back a tear and stifled a sniffle to hide it from her children. Everything that had been taken from her was being outlined so cruelly by this trip.

Still, the hours did pass, and they disembarked at the station in their old home. It seemed to Chana that everything should have changed because she had changed so much, but the streets were the same. They walked past the building that used to be a synagogue. It was now a church, and the beautiful stained-glass windows she remembered in front had been replaced with images of Jesus hanging from the cross. The windows had been destroyed the night of Kristallnacht, she remembered. After a few more minutes of walking, they turned down the street that led to their home.

The area had once been almost solely Jewish. The Kranzwitz family had owned the house on the corner with the big front yard, but they had all died in the Ghetto. The large Goldschmidt family had lived in three houses along the row, built one after another as each generation married and had a large brood of children. Chana didn't remember ever seeing them in the Ghetto; she had no idea what had happened to them. And, finally, they arrived at her own house.

It had been Zayde and Bubbie's house, but they had retired to a single room on the first floor when their age got the better of them. Father and Mother had kept up the house when Father's brothers had moved to the city and his sister had married the Goldblat's oldest son. Chana had grown up in the house and given birth to all four of her sons there. She and her husband had been saving their funds to purchase an empty plot of land down the street to begin building their own home, but those dreams were long gone now.

Yakov strode forward and knocked on the front door, a door he had probably never had to wait for entry at before. A woman opened the door after a few long moments. She was covered in flour from baking, but Chana thought she recognized her from the goy schoolchildren she had grown up with.

"Go away," the woman snapped. "Your kind aren't welcome here."

"We're not here to reclaim our house," Yakov snapped in return. "You can keep what you have stolen. All we want are our belongings, if any still remain."

She wouldn't have let them in. She was probably about to disappear inside to call the police. But then her oldest son appeared behind her apron strings.

"Gideon?" the boy asked. "You're Gideon."

Chana knew where she remembered the woman. There was a park a few blocks down the street, situated in between the Jewish neighborhood and the goy one. They had both taken their children to play there, and as only good mothers could, they'd ignored the fact that their sons were playing together on occasion.

"Hello, Franz," Gideon replied softly.

"Well, don't just stand there looking like dirty thieves," the woman snapped. She ushered them inside and stomped into the foyer. "Don't think I'll allow you to take whatever you please," she added over her shoulder.

She followed them room to room as they searched. Bubbie's room was first, where they hoped to find her wedding pearls. Those were gone. In fact, all of their belongings were gone. The furniture was different; the clothes all belonged to someone else. Chana's prized china doll was absent from its prominent place in the windowsill in her bedroom. They only thing remaining was mother's wedding dress, tucked into an unassuming box in a corner of the attic. Chana took it with her when they left. The front door slammed behind them, and the lock clicked shut with finality. That chapter of their lives was over.

The walk back to the train station was a heavy one. None of the heirlooms had been there. Chana had hoped they would have been saved from the trash heap because of their value in silver, but they were gone.

"Chana, wait," Yakov said suddenly. She stopped walking and turned to look where Yakov was pointing. In the window of a chandler's shop was a display of candles, and holding those candles were her bubbie's prized silver Shabbat candlesticks.

Yakov walked into the shop while Chana waited outside. Ten minutes later, she could see the shopkeeper in the window taking the candlesticks down from the display. It was another five minutes before Yakov emerged holding a large wrapped package.

"The hanukiah was in there too," he explained, gently patting the package.

Magnified

"Was the Seder plate there?" Chana asked. All three silver pieces were a matched set, bought by her great-great-grandparents for their wedding.

"The shop keep said he hadn't seen it. I'll keep looking, but we should hurry if we want to catch the next train."

They managed to get on the proper train heading to the port, and for the next three days, Chana tried to relax and keep her family happy. Yakov was tense from being so far away from Martin. Chana was worried about the journey ahead and what America would bring in the future. The children were picking up on the adults' discomfort and were beginning to get fussy on the last day of the trip.

The train pulled into the port station in the early afternoon. Yakov hurried off to find the proper office where their visas were waiting while Chana took the children to look at the ocean.

"It's so big!" Aharon gasped. "We're really going to cross it?"

"Oh yes," Chana replied. "It will be a fun adventure." It would be something new and different, so far removed from the life she was leaving behind that it honestly didn't matter to her what struggles she would have to endure in the future. Nothing could be worse than the Ghetto.

Yakov returned with the tickets and the visas. Chana cringed at how much money they must have cost Martin to get arranged so quickly. Yakov had gotten directions to the correct berth and led the way to the gigantic steam ship. It had a full head of steam already going.

"It's leaving in an hour," Yakov explained. "You should board now."

He hugged each of her children one at a time, explaining patiently to Aharon that he wasn't going with them. He gave

Shimon a long kiss on the forehead before passing him back over to Chana. He hugged Chana last.

"Be safe over there," he whispered into her ear. "And find some happiness."

She hugged Yakov back tightly with one arm. "If Martin ever causes you problems, come to America too. There will always be a place for you in my home."

"I'll miss you, Chana," he said as he slowly drew away.

Chana walked up the gangway with purposeful steps. She handed the tickets over to the sailor waiting at the top and was given directions to find a spot below deck in the cargo hold. Instead, she stood by the railing to watch the docks where Yakov was still standing. As dusk settled over the port and the sailors began untying the ropes holding the ship in place, a shadow fell over Yakov. He looked up, and she could see him smile and reach out to take Martin's hand.

She didn't bother to dwell on how Martin had gotten to the docks so quickly, instead focusing on Yakov's visible happiness. Then the ship pulled away from the docks and she couldn't see them any longer, so Chana gathered her children to go find a place to sleep.

2004

"And so I arrived in America with four children, my mother's wedding dress, a pair of candlesticks, a hanukiah, and some small coins Martin was kind enough to provide," Gramma finished. "They called me Hannah at Ellis Island. Can you believe that? How difficult is Chana to spell in English? But I didn't argue because they almost sent Shmuley back to Poland when he sneezed while we were in line for the physical." That was a story Yani had heard dozens of times. About the little bit of dust that had gotten them moved to a more invasive medical screening line. Gramma used to make fun of Great-uncle Shmuley any time he sneezed where she could hear it, but the mixture of fond reproach she always colored her words with turned what Yani knew was a moment of extreme stress into a humorous anecdote. "There were more important things to worry about than getting my name right. They got Shmuley's name wrong too. But somehow we prevailed, and now I have my family around me as my life comes to an end. How could I ask for something more?"

"But what happened to Yakov?" Yani asked curiously.

Gramma let out a tired laugh. "I couldn't say. He never came to America to visit. But let me tell you a secret. Ten years ago, I received a package in the mail from Poland. It was from an address I did not recognize, but I opened it anyway. Inside the package was my grandmother's lost Seder plate. Someone had found it and returned it to me, but the only person still in Europe who knew it was missing was Yakov. I think he and Martin are alive and well."

"You're saying you met a vampire?" one of the married-in relatives scoffed. "Couldn't you just tell us the truth about how you survived the Holocaust?"

Gramma smiled gently. "Believe what you will, but I know what happened. I sent a letter to that address in Poland the day before I was hospitalized. I knew what was coming, and I wanted to make sure Yakov did too. If you see him at my funeral, please ask him if he's still happy."

Yani and Shira were taken home soon afterward. They had bedtimes to keep to, and even Gramma dying couldn't stop that. The phone rang in the middle of the night. Yani crept to his bedroom door and cracked it open so he could hear into his parents' room down the hall.

"Thank you for telling me, Daddy," Mom was saying. "I'll make sure Yani and Shira understand in the morning."

Gramma had passed away peacefully in her sleep during the night.

T he funeral was held three days later.

Yani was stuffed into a suit and tie. It itched and made him feel strangled, but Gramma had always liked how sharp and adult he looked all dressed up. It made a sad sort of sense to wear the outfit for her one last time.

According to Gramma's will, the funeral service needed to be in the afternoon. Gramma's family and friends all squeezed into the small chapel attached to the funeral home. Shira had to sit in Mom's lap, but Yani was able to get his own seat.

The wooden coffin was closed. It was dark wood with bright flowers on top. Gramma had always liked pinks and oranges, colors she couldn't see while in the Ghetto. Grandpa Gideon hadn't skimped, even though flowers at a Jewish funeral were superfluous.

The rabbi led afternoon prayers first. Yani followed along in the siddur, but his eyes kept straying back to the coffin. Was Gramma happy in heaven? Had she met up with her husband from Poland, killed in the Ghetto, or with her rabbi husband from America who had passed away from a stroke twenty years ago? Maybe her husbands were fighting over her. Yani had to hide a totally inappropriate laugh at the thought. Gramma would laugh at them both, and Yani didn't doubt that her smile would appease her husbands until some sort of compromise could be made.

When the service was over, the rabbi said some nice words about Gramma: how she attended nearly every Saturday morning service, was active in the synagogue's women's network. How everyone loved Gramma.

Grandpa Gideon spoke next about the time Gramma had sewn a hem for a rich lady and had gotten an extra tip. "She bought penny candies for all four children," he said, his voice choked even as he manfully continued to speak. "Instead of saving the money or putting it toward her goal of moving out of the city, she instead gave us a little moment of happiness. Mother was like that, trying to make everyone happy."

Uncle Aharon spoke next, and then Uncle Shmuley. They told their own stories and memories of what had made Gramma so special. Then Uncle Shimon stepped forward.

"Chana wasn't actually my mother by birth," he began softly. "But that never mattered. In fact, I never knew until I was in high school and we had to fill out a genealogy form for some science class. She welcomed me into her arms as if I were her youngest son in truth with smiles and tenderness. I can't imagine what raising me was like, the hardship she took on to care for an infant on top of her own children. Not once did her smile waver. She never complained or griped. Quite simply, she loved us all equally. She was my mother, and I'm going to miss her."

Aunt Miriam and Aunt Ariela, Gramma's last two children, stepped forward together to share a prewritten speech about Gramma. They needed to keep switching who was reading when one broke down crying midway. Once they had returned to their seats, the rabbi said a few more words and then led the closing prayers of mourning. "Yitgadal v'yit kadash sh'may raba," they all chanted together. (Magnified and sanctified be G-d's great name.)

Then the men of the family all stepped forward to lift Gramma's coffin into the air. They led the way out of the chapel and through the funeral home to the parking lot where a black hearse was waiting.

Yani helped Shira get her car seat buckled in their own car. The sun was setting behind them as Dad drove in the long procession of cars behind the hearse. The drive wasn't a lengthy one. Yani saw the Jewish Star hanging in welcome above the entrance to the cemetery before Dad slotted the car into a parking spot.

The coffin was already resting above the hole in the ground that would be Gramma's grave, held in place by firm straps. Once everyone was assembled, the rabbi said a few more words, and then the straps began to lower the coffin into the ground. Two cemetery employees were there to pull away the straps, and then they left.

"Let us say our final goodbyes to Chana Herzstein," the rabbi intoned solemnly. "It is difficult to say goodbye, and we are reluctant to do so. In order to convey this, we turn the shovel over and pick up some dirt with the back. Then we turn the shovel right side up and add two more scoops to honor Chana." The rabbi did as instructed, first picking up a little dirt with the back of the shovel and gently tossing it into the hole in the ground. She added two more scoops to the deep grave and then stuck the shovel back into the pile of dirt. The dirt made an echoing thump as it hit the coffin lid, but as everyone lined up to add their own shovelfuls, the echo eventually subsided.

The barest sliver of sunlight remained in the sky when Yani stepped forward to add some dirt to Gramma's grave. Aunties Miriam and Ariela were sobbing softly into tissues, and Uncle Shimon's face was screwed up as if he were barely managing to hold back his own tears. Yani's three shovelfuls of dirt trickled into the grave one by one, and then he stepped aside to let someone else have a turn.

The line eventually diminished, and the family moved away from the grave to give last hugs to each other. Many of them would be at Grandpa Gideon's house in just a half hour for shivah to begin, Yani included, but he let his older cousins that he hadn't seen in a while give him hugs anyway.

Only the streetlights lit up the cemetery by the time people started heading to their cars. Yani turned for one last look at the grave and stopped short. There were two people he didn't recognize standing there. One was holding the shovel, and as Yani watched, he added three careful scoops of dirt to the grave. For some reason, Yani felt drawn to the two figures. He started walking back toward the grave, past Grandpa Gideon who had turned to stare incredulously at the two figures saying goodbye to Gramma.

The strains of the Mourner's Kaddish, chanted solemnly and with reverence, reached Yani's ears as he drew close. *Yitgadal v'yit kadash sh'may raba…* He stopped walking a respectful distance away while both figures stood hand in hand until the Kaddish was complete. Then they both turned to look at Yani.

The shorter figure looked a lot like the grainy pictures of Uncle Shimon from fifty years ago. Mom always said that Yani had gotten his good looks from Gramma's side of the family, but he had never realized that all those times Gramma had looked in his direction with a fond smile and vacant eyes that weren't quite focused on him that she had been remembering her brother. Yani looked very similar to Yakov, despite the fact that he still had years of growing up to still do.

Standing next to Yakov was a tall man with pale hair and bright-blue eyes. Yani wouldn't have recognized him without Gramma's story. Yakov and Martin looked like they were both younger than Mom, but Yani knew Yakov was supposed to be almost as old as Gramma.

"Gramma said to ask if you were still happy, Uncle Yakov," Yani said finally, once his perusal of the two vampires was complete. With Gramma's story still fresh in his mind, he never even thought that he should be afraid.

Yakov glanced over his shoulder at Martin, who was hovering close by. Martin quirked an eyebrow at Yakov, and Yakov couldn't stop a wide smile from blooming across his face.

"Oh, Chana," he laughed, smiling down at his older sister's grave. "Yes. Yes, I'm still happy. And it's good to know you had a happy life too."

Yani watched as Yakov reached out to take the hand Martin had already held out to him. Between the blink of an eye, they were gone and Yani turned around to walk back to his waiting family. He stopped suddenly and glanced back down at Gramma's grave.

"See, Gramma," Yani explained. "Everyone is happy. Thank you."

A year after Chana's death, Yakov insisted they travel back to the United States to visit her grave. Martin made the arrangements, glad for the convenience of planes with windowless cargo holds. They never could have made the trip across the Atlantic in a ship. They sealed themselves up in packing boxes, had a friend deliver them to the post office, and mailed themselves to a modest Upstate New York home Martin had acquired the previous year for the same purpose.

Yakov held tightly to Martin's hand as they entered the cemetery exactly one year after Chana had been buried. It was dark outside, clouds skittering across the sky to hide the stars and the moon. They didn't need light to see the graves spread throughout the cemetery, but Yakov still walked at a slow, human pace along the path until they reached Chana's grave.

The grass was oddly flattened around the grave, as if a large number of people had been by to visit recently. The grave itself had an even layer of grass over it, neatly mown as if the grave had been part of the cemetery for an entire decade instead of a mere year. At the head of the grave, where a year ago had been only a large pile of dirt waiting to cover Chana's coffin forever, was a shiny new tombstone.

Chana bat Miriam, it read in English and Hebrew. Chana, daughter of Miriam. It listed her estimated birth year of 1913 and her death year of 2004. Below that, an intricate Jewish Star had been carved.

Yakov dug into his pocket and pulled out a stone from their garden back home. He gently placed the rock next to a pile of other rocks on top of the tombstone and then stepped back into Martin's chest.

Martin immediately wrapped his arms around Yakov, knowing his beloved was seeking comfort.

"I'll always remember you," Yakov whispered, "and the life you allowed me to have. Most sisters would have run screaming the second they met Martin." He laughed, a choked sound that belied his dry eyes. "A male goy and a vampire? You should have dragged me onto the boat to America with you. I'm so glad you didn't."

He looked one last time at the rock he had left on Chana's tombstone. It wouldn't wither or fade like a flower. No, it would last for as long as Yakov's memories of Chana would last. Martin held out one hand, and Yakov gripped it tightly as they turned and left the cemetery. Chana was gone, but her legacy would live on for decades to come.

One:Truth

2012

Someone had drawn a Hitler mustache on the face of the President of the United States. It was a political statement, meant to equate the president's policies with socialism and Nazism. There were people pointing and laughing while others just shook their heads in exasperation at yet another Republican/Tea Party rally on the street corner.

Yani had frozen in shock, staring helplessly as poster after poster was paraded around in a circle as the protest continued unimpeded. Acid churned in the pit of his stomach, and he had to force bile back down his throat as a woman holding one of the posters yelled happily about the evils of the president.

He didn't care about what perceived ill they thought the president had committed. Nor did he care about whether the protest was justified. All he could see was that black, miniature mustache plastered under the president's nose.

Didn't they know what they were saying? Those protesters who equated the president to Hitler? They couldn't know. They couldn't know about the millions of dead people, the Aryanism, the selective sterilizations. They hadn't seen the pictures of dead children, their thin bodies more bone than flesh, or the mass graves where bodies of Jews shot mercilessly in the woods and fields had been tossed aside like trash. Innocent people dead, their only crime being different from Hitler's ideal human.

How could an intelligent, thinking person equate the president with something so heinous and then laugh about it? Or think they were justified? Whatever perceived wrongs the president was committing, he would never reach the sheer evil of Hitler, and the comparison was oh so very wrong.

"They're just ignorant fools," Mary insisted. "One day they'll pay for their stupidity and lies." She yanked on Yani's arm to force him to start walking again. "Don't pay them any mind."

Yani sighed. There wasn't anything he could do. Going over and yelling at them wouldn't stop them, nor would calmly trying to explain why what they were doing was wrong. The protesters thought they were ideologically right and therefore above reproach; they wouldn't listen to Yani's words.

He tightened his grip on his suitcase and followed Mary away from them. Even once he turned a corner and couldn't see them, Yani was still fuming. He and Mary finally reached the T stop. They stopped together outside the turnstiles.

"Have a good holiday," Mary insisted. "Eat lots of apples and honey and whatnot. I'll email you a copy of my class notes."

"I'll be back in a few days," Yani insisted. "Rosh Hashanah is only a two-day holiday."

Magnified

Mary snorted in disbelief and gave a negative shake of her head. "I've seen your schedule this month. First Rosh Hashanah, then Yom Kippur, Sukkot, and a bunch of other holidays I can't even begin to pronounce. If you don't have my notes, you'll miss too much."

Yani just sighed. They only shared two classes this semester, and Yani was only traveling home for the High Holidays—Rosh Hashanah and then Yom Kippur the following week. Not only was he barely missing class, but after three full years at college, he knew to arrange extra study sessions with his professors ahead of time to catch up on the missed work. Still, that was Mary; she always wanted to help.

"Thanks," he finally replied. "I'll see you in a few days." Yani tapped his Charlie Card on the turnstile machine and then yanked his suitcase through behind him once it beeped to tell him he had paid.

"I'll try to find you a new boyfriend for when you come back!" Mary called over the noise of the busy station.

Yani spun around, nearly tripping himself, to glare at her. "Please don't!"

Mary grinned evilly and then waved once before turning around and heading back into the city proper. Yani had to hurry to catch the T so he wouldn't be late. He took the green line to the Park Street stop and then switched to the red line. The red line took him to South Station, which was a gigantic transportation station with connections to city bus routes, commuter rail trains, and after a quick walk through the traffic of people and down one of the lengthy platforms for a waiting commuter rail train, Yani reached the bus station.

He could see the archway declaring the entrance to Boston's Chinatown through the large glass windows in the front of the bus station as he walked toward the escalator. The escalator led to a large lobby, the purpose of which Yani had never figured out. He walked through the lobby and to another escalator that finally brought him up to the station proper. At the top of the escalator was the cordoned-off space to buy tickets, so Yani got in line.

Boston, for all that it was a modern, bustling city, was really a college town. Yani could count dozens of colleges scattered throughout the city, and entire T lines were organized based on where the colleges were located. The B Line on the Green Line first stopped a half dozen times for Boston University students and then hooked sharply in order to terminate at Boston College. The Red Line connected MIT and UMass to the rest of the city as well, which still left out all the small colleges with T stops scattered around the city.

The Greyhound station was always packed with college students heading home during holidays, but at the end of September with school just begun, the station was practically empty. Yani only had to wait for one couple ahead of him before he could buy his ticket, and the line for his bus had a total of five people waiting in it. Even the bus, when it finally arrived ten minutes late, was barely half-full. Yani didn't have to share his double seat, which was wonderful.

"Thank you for choosing Greyhound," the bus driver said politely into the intercom as he backed the bus away from the station. "This is the Greyhound bus to Albany, New York, with stops at Riverside and Worcester. The trip should take approximately three and a half hours with an estimated arrival time at 3:05 p.m. Please keep cell phone conversations brief and quiet and your music down low. Thank you for choosing Greyhound," he repeated before falling silent.

The bus pulled onto the highway and was off. The Riverside stop was only a ten-minute drive away, just on the other side of Boston. The Worcester stop was farther. On really busy days, and if Yani was lucky, he could get a nonstop bus straight to Albany, but it was a slow day so he made do.

He pulled one of his textbooks from his backpack and settled in to read that week's assignment. In just a few hours he would be home, and as much as he enjoyed college, there was nothing quite like home.

"Why can't Yani get his own car?" Shira whined. "Why do we have to go out of our way to pick him up?"

"Having a car in Boston is like being a Yankees fan in Boston: stupid and possibly detrimental to your health," Yani replied, rehashing an old argument repeated every time Shira was schlepped along to pick him up. The streets in Boston were like any busy city street: too many cars with impatient drivers careening down the narrow roads. It was a potential deadly traffic accident waiting to happen, and Yani didn't want to even attempt bringing a car there. Shira was sitting in the back seat, pouting because she had never been able to win that argument. "How are your bat-mitzvah lessons going, anyway?"

"Shut up, Yani," Shira snapped. Not so well, then. She was only eleven, but the amount of preparation that went into leading the service was intense; she needed the extra two years of practice if she wanted to do as much of the service as Yani had.

"That's enough, both of you," Dad said. He was concentrating on getting through the Albany streets to the highway. The Albany Greyhound station was a dump in need of massive renovation. The building was old and literally falling down a little more every time Yani was there, and the parking lot was in desperate need of new pavement. The station was also not located in the best of neighborhoods, but after three years of practice, Dad knew how to pick up Yani and get home quickly with minimum fuss. It only took a few minutes to get on the highway and head out of the city to the Albany suburbs.

Home was a two-story cookie-cutter house with an attached two-car garage and a good bit of land. Dad parked in the garage, and Yani climbed out with his bag in hand. Shira had already stomped her way into the house. The displaced air from the door wafted delicious smells of roasting chicken, chicken soup, kugel, and, of course, apples. Rosh Hashanah was the celebration of the start of a new year, and the common saying among friends and family was "May you have a good and sweet year." Eating apples dipped in honey to symbolize that fervent wish was the tradition that went along with that saying.

"Oh, good. You're back," Mom called. She and two of Yani's aunts were sweating in the heat of the kitchen as they put together the celebratory feast. "Finish setting the table, please."

Yani couldn't stop a smile from tugging at his lips at the sheer normality of it all. Despite his return from college, he wasn't treated as a guest or a stranger. It wasn't his family's way. He quickly jogged upstairs to deposit his bag on his neatly made bed and then hurried back downstairs just in time to take a stack of china from his father. The dining room table had already been expanded to its full length, and two more tables had been added to the end. Tablecloths and glass drinking cups were neatly laid out. Yani began to carefully set each delicate plate in front of each glass.

He returned to the kitchen when he was done and was put to the task of carrying fragile wineglasses—only two at a time, or his mom would yell—to the table. He could hear Shira grumbling to herself from the laundry room down the hall as she cleaned the silver in the utility sink there.

It took a good hour to finish setting the table, especially once Grandpa Gideon and Uncle Shmuley took seats near the head and had to stop Yani and Shira to chat every time they reappeared carrying dishes and silver. Eventually all that was left was finding extra chairs.

They carted the kitchen chairs in first and then the folding chairs up from the basement. Yani counted place settings and chairs and had to hide a hopeful grin. They were exactly one chair short, which wasn't enough to send one of the aunts or uncles home for their extras.

"There's still the chair in the study," Yani reminded his dad when they both stood at the final place setting without a chair, wondering when the missing one had gotten broken.

His dad sighed. "I know. I'll go get it." He reached into his pocket for the key.

"Mike, can you get this bowl down for me?" Yani's mom called at the perfect moment.

Dad grimaced. "She can't even wait until I finish one thing before starting me on something else." He pressed the key into Yani's hand and hurried off.

Yani had to keep himself from doing a little jig in place. He hurried to the door to the study and unlocked it before slowly stepping inside and shut the door behind him.

His parents weren't hiding anything important in their study, nor were they purposefully keeping anyone out. When Shira was five, she had wanted to explore and had not only shredded her way through half of Dad's important work documents, but had nearly broken Gramma's prized hanukiah when she'd pulled it down from the shelf. Dad had put a lock on the door the next day, but had only realized after he had managed to lock himself out without the key two days later that it automatically relocked whenever the door closed. Luckily, jimmying the lock with a screwdriver had let Dad recover the keys that day. Somehow the lock had never gotten changed again, and Yani could count on one hand the number of times he had ever been in the room.

It felt almost sacrilegious to be in the study, especially by himself, but Yani had been waiting for the chance for over two years. The last time he had been in the office, he and Dad had been looking for his college payment receipt to show the health-insurance company. Yani had pulled open a drawer and found an envelope with his Gramma's cramped cursive on the outside. A quick peek inside had shown a handwritten address to somewhere in Poland, but then his dad had found the document and Yani had left before he understood just whom that address belonged to.

Yani's fingers were shaking slightly as he pulled open that same drawer in the desk. Nestled in the back of the drawer was the same cream-colored envelope, and inside was the address. Yani quickly pulled out his iPhone and typed the address into his contacts. Then he carefully shut the drawer and got the extra chair from the corner.

Dinner that night, as with any family dinner, was loud and happy. They said the requisite blessings over candles, wine, apples, and challah, and then Mom and the aunts brought out the gefilte-fish plates for appetizer.

"So, how's school going?" Aunty Miriam asked as she passed the horseradish to him. Almost immediately, Yani found himself the center of attention. The semester had barely started, but he had attended each class at least twice, so he started outlining his syllabi. He was taking a math class to fulfill that school requirement. Grandpa Gideon immediately latched on to that, asking all sorts of questions that Yani didn't really want to answer. He didn't particularly like math, and the class was definitely for nonmajors. Aunt Ariela and her oldest daughter, Aunt Marge—both lawyers—were interested in his political-science class on human rights, which was a much more interesting subject. Talking about his subjects got them through the soup course. Yani let out a little sigh of relief when attention turned to Shira's middle-school classes and the beginning of the college search for one of Yani's cousins.

It wasn't that he didn't like talking with his family, but his iPhone was burning a hole in his pocket. He didn't know what he wanted to write to Yakov, or if he even would, but ever since they had briefly met at Gramma's funeral, Yani wanted to know more about his undead uncle.

Even the sheer idea of having a vampire in the family was boggling. Sometimes Yani wondered if he had imagined the encounter at Gramma's graveside. He had been young, and maybe he wasn't remembering correctly. Maybe he had met another uncle, one who had moved away from the rest of the family and wasn't spoken about much. One who was born in the 1990s, and that was why the man had looked so young.

But Yani also remembered Gramma's story and the fierceness in her eyes as she spoke of her younger brother, Yakov, as he remained behind to stay with a lover who drank blood for survival. Gramma hadn't been lying, and Yani didn't think his eyes had deceived him all those years ago either.

"So Rakhél's new boyfriend is a goy. Oy vey! He will not last too long, I hope," Auntie Anna, Miriam's third daughter, sighed with a pointedly raised eyebrow at Rakhél's blushing face.

"She's just in high school," Auntie Miriam scolded. "You dated a goy in high school too, you remember. Don't think I've forgotten catching you both coming back from a *Rocky Horror* show kissing in the back of his car."

"And yet you still kept peeking through the blinds every time I came home from a date," Auntie Anna sighed.

"Until you brought home a boy I approved of," Miriam grumped, glancing over at Uncle Jay, who was grinning happily at the two women.

"So what about you, Yani?" Auntie Anne said suddenly, clearly eager to change the conversation away from her past love life. "Any nice Jewish boyfriends to speak of?"

Yani sighed. He had come out to his family in high school, and no one had blinked. Gramma had raised her children well; being open and welcoming was central in her beliefs. Yani hadn't been afraid to come out of the closet, but occasionally he regretted having a sexuality at all. As nearly every face turned in his direction, eagerly awaiting a new bit of gossip to harangue Yani over, Yani knew he was experiencing one of those times.

"Mary's planning to set me up on another blind date," Yani finally said after a long moment when the stares grew more anticipatory. "The last boy just wanted to play video games all day." And have lots of sex, but he wasn't telling his family that part, particularly since the sex hadn't always happened with Yani. The breakup hadn't been pretty, and Yani was just glad it was over.

"Wasn't Mary's last blind date that scary punk rocker with all those tattoos?" Mom asked tentatively from her seat of honor closest to the kitchen door. She was hiding a grimace because Yani had actually liked Luke's appearance despite her disapproval. He had been fun to hang out with, and the sex had been fantastic, but Yani'd had to put his foot down when Luke's cheating came to his attention.

"She promised me she would find someone normal next time," Yani replied with a shrug. Mary was his friend, and he appreciated her looking out for him. He just wished it didn't bring his family's worries down on his head. Everyone in the world pointed to their own culture and explained how they had learned to worry so well, but no one heaped on worry like a Jewish mother. The phone calls he'd gotten when Mom had happened to see him kissing Luke in a picture on Facebook—Yani didn't particularly want to think about it.

Magnified

Luckily, Grandpa Gideon demanded dessert, and the conversation ended as the dinner plates were cleared and replaced with dessert plates. Coffee and tea were served along with an apple cake and rugelach, but as soon as dessert was finished, the aunts and uncles with younger kids started making noise about heading home. They were then echoed by anyone who didn't want to get stuck with helping to clean up. Twenty minutes later, the last hug was given and the front door shut behind the final guest.

Of course, Yani would see every single one of them in synagogue the next morning and again that night for the second Rosh Hashanah dinner. From the tight hug from Grandpa Gideon to his youngest cousins, a pair of five-year-old twins, insisting that Yani give them kisses—Yani was familied out and he had only been home a few short hours.

The dishwasher was already full and running by the time Yani caught his breath at the door and went in search of Mom. She pointed wordlessly toward the dining room, her hand dripping soap onto the floor from the delicate china she was handwashing. Yani found Dad there, clearing one table at a time so he could get to the tablecloths which desperately needed presoaking in spot remover. Shira was following behind Dad with cleaning spray to ensure the tables themselves were clean once the tablecloths were removed.

Yani jumped in, picking up the piles of dishes his dad had made and carting them into the kitchen for his mom to clean. The counters filled up quickly, much faster than Mom could make the dishes vanish, but before long the dining room was back to its normal, everyday emptiness. Yani couldn't tell a party had recently occurred in the space, which meant Mom wouldn't yell when she came over to inspect.

It was late by then. Midnight had come and gone. Shira headed off to bed, but Yani was conscripted to dry and put away the clean handwashables. By the time he finally climbed into his childhood bed, all he could do was gather the covers under his chin and fall immediately to sleep, thoughts of the address burning a hole in his cell phone completely forgotten.

The rest of the holiday passed quickly. The traditions and celebrations of Rosh Hashanah didn't change from year to year. They were set in stone religiously, and his family had been celebrating in their own personal way for so long that switching something around would just feel wrong and unpleasant.

The next morning Yani was woken by Dad yelling up the stairs that breakfast was ready. Shira beat him downstairs for pancakes, but Yani ate faster so was able to commandeer the shower first. Afterward, he put on a suit and tie, combed his hair, found his tallit bag, and joined Dad downstairs to wait for the ladies to find their shoes and the other half-dozen things they needed to do to get ready in the morning.

Sometimes Yani wondered if that was why he was gay—he had no patience for women—but then he would catch his dad rolling his eyes as Mom and Shira snapped at each other over skirt length and too much eye makeup and wonder if it was just a guy thing instead of a gay thing.

Services were always boring. That was just how it was. Yani sat in an uncomfortable chair, brushing shoulders with his dad on one side while trying to figure out why the old lady on his other side thought perfume was an acceptable substitute for a bath. The rest of the family was ranged around them, taking up a fairly large section of seats in multiple rows. The rabbi led the service from the bimah, and when it was over Yani went home for a traditional lunch of leftovers.

That afternoon was the slichot service, where all the sins of the past year were symbolically cast away in order to prepare for the new year. Yani tossed his stale bread into the local river while the rabbi led yet another service on freeing oneself from the sins of the past and reminding the congregation that Yom Kippur was fast approaching.

Dinner that night was at Uncle Joe's house, and services the next morning were a boring repeat. All too soon, Yani found himself back on a Greyhound bus heading to Boston. He pulled out another textbook to catch up on some of the material he had missed and settled in for the long ride up the Mass Pike.

Yani brought his laptop to the dining hall for dinner. Two of his professors had uploaded their PowerPoints from the classes he had missed, and there was wireless for him to download them. Catching up on work was better than looking like he didn't have any friends to eat with, but Mary and Ettie were both in class for another half hour and Tony was spending the night over at BC with his girlfriend. Plus, there was food and plenty of coffee readily available to bolster his studying.

His human rights professor had apparently begun explaining the twenty-page final project hinted at in the syllabus. Yani scrolled through the PowerPoint slowly, reading the lines that caught his eye and checking for any of the professor's notes in the footnotes as he went. The final slide outlined the project. He had to write a paper about a genocide, investigating not just the cause and the terrible events that occurred, but the political situation in the country in question and the world as a whole that allowed the genocide to transpire.

The Holocaust topped the list, of course, but it wasn't a small list either. Rwanda was there, as were the Ukrainian, Armenian, and Chilean genocides. The professor had added a note to the slide, stating that a student had already requested to do his project on the Trail of Tears, which wasn't on the original list.

Yani frowned down at the list, wondering which one he should choose. The Holocaust would be the easy choice. Not only had Yani grown up learning all about the six million of his people who had been so brutally murdered, but Gramma had given him a personal connection to the horror of the times. It would actually be harder to find resources to support the knowledge that was already in his head than to just write the essay. But in a way it felt like cheating; it was too damn easy. He should study the Ukrainian genocide instead and learn all about the Holodomor.

Besides, Yani remembered with a start, his family's holocaust story was colored by supernatural events that he ought to keep secret. And, Yani also remembered he had the means to contact said supernatural creatures.

He had totally forgotten. Yani grimaced while shaking his head furiously. How had he forgotten? But then the holidays were pretty crazy.

Yani abandoned his homework and opened up a blank Word document. He stared at the page for a few long minutes. How did he begin a letter to his undead uncle? Should he even be writing to Uncle Yakov? Mom would certainly yell if she found out, but Yani couldn't understand why no one had bothered to keep Yakov in the loop where the family was concerned. He was their uncle, and Yakov had loved them enough to see them safely away from Europe. Why wouldn't he want to know how they were?

Yani took a bite of his sandwich and chewed for a few long moments before resolutely putting his fingers over the letters on his keyboard.

Dear Uncle Yakov and Uncle Martin, he wrote, knowing that was the easiest way to start a letter. *This past Rosh Hashanah I stole your mailing address from my mother. She was entrusted with it when Great-grandmother Chana died. I don't think Mom's been writing to you, but I thought you might enjoy knowing how the family is doing. I guess I'll start with me, since I'm writing the letter. I will get to Gramma Chana next, and Uncle Shimon too, don't worry.*

My name is Yani Goldhaber. My mom is Grandpa Gideon's third child. You and I met at Gramma Chana's funeral.

Yani didn't know what else to write. How did he explain who he was to a man he had barely met?

"You've been avoiding me," Mary admonished as she plopped down in the chair across from Yani. "Back at school for four hours, and I haven't heard from you once!"

Yani quickly saved his letter and the PowerPoint before closing his computer and safely stowing it away in his bag. "I had a class that just got out and so did you," Yani replied with a frown.

"Yeah, yeah," Mary sighed with an absentminded wave of her hand. "Semantics. Don't bore me with them. Anyway." She leaned forward conspiratorially and a wide grin split her face. "I've found you the perfect boy."

"Mary," Yani groaned. "I told you not to set me up on any more blind dates."

"I'm sure you did," she agreed, "but Aaron is perfect for you. He's hot beyond all belief"—she fanned her hand in front of her face as if she were cooling herself down—"and he's a good person. He teaches the football program at Charlie's Hand."

Charlie's Hand was a nonprofit organization meant to help underprivileged children learn and grow in a safe and welcoming environment. Mary taught the cheerleading section there, which not only entailed teaching her kids cheerleading moves and teamwork, but also included time for homework and help with studying. Yani lauded her for participating in such a great program, but he couldn't join her. He tried to stay away from programs touting working hand in hand with Jesus. He couldn't uphold the values the organization was trying to promote to the children, nor could he understand it. Yani did his community service elsewhere.

"Mary, if I date another non-Jew so soon after Luke, my mother will have an apoplexy."

"Oh, hush," she scoffed. "Aaron's Jewish. One of those Reform types that believes more in assimilation than Judaism. I think he grew up attending a Unitarian Universalist Church, but he told me his mom was never really happy there since she grew up a little more stringently."

"Mary, is he really Jewish? As in, I won't be lying to my mom when I tell her about it later?"

Mary nodded and she grinned. "And he's hot, Yani. If he weren't gay, I'd already be dating him."

"Fine," Yani sighed. "Give me the time and place, and I'll meet with him."

"Yay!" Mary giggled.

"What's yay?" Ettie asked as she dropped a heavy tray of food onto the table. Yani rescued his computer bag from the resulting spill and returned to his sandwich while Mary turned her attention to scolding Ettie.

Mary and Ettie were as opposite looking as two people could be, but they were also best friends. They were one of the very few examples of the freshman roommate-pairing system actually working. Yani shuddered to remember his own freshman roommate; his belongings had smelled like pot for weeks after the guy had been arrested and expelled for dealing crack on campus. But Mary and Ettie had bonded from day one and had never looked back.

Mary was thin with a neat bob of light-brown hair framing a pixie-shaped face. Ettie, on the other hand, was proud of her plus-sized body and confident in her exotic good looks. Ettie had shaved her head at the beginning of the semester and was just starting to grow back a fuzz of black spikes. The black choker around her neck complemented her black chunky bracelet and coordinating watchband.

"Fine, I'll clean it up!" Ettie snapped before stomping away to the nearest napkin dispenser. Mary rescued the still edible items on the tray, and Ettie cleaned up the spill. They both vanished for a few minutes afterward to get more food, Ettie a second full tray and Mary a leafy green salad with sliced chicken in it.

"So, what were we talking about?" Mary asked after she sat across from Yani and started eating.

"Date and time," Yani sighed, starting to wonder why he had decided to wait in such a conspicuous place for his friends to find him. They drove him crazy more often than not—but then that was what college friends were for.

"Duh, the coffee shop at six tomorrow. Same place and time as last time."

"Seriously, Mary? What if I run into Luke there?" Yani shook his head, trying to hide his grimace. His relationship with Luke had ended less than amicably, and Yani wasn't interested in falling back into bed with him while he was supposedly on a blind date with another guy. It had happened before when Yani had just stopped in to get coffee and Luke had offered a fun night together, but Yani wasn't going to do that again.

"Don't you trust me?" Mary gasped theatrically. "Luke has class until seven thirty. And, hey—" She paused, giving Yani a small grin. "—if this date goes badly, too, I'll spring for enough Jell-O shots that you won't care who you go home with that night. You'll have a good lay and we can start over in the morning."

"Ugh, Mary," Yani groaned.

"Yeah, ugh," Ettie agreed between bites of her sandwich. "So how's that essay coming?"

"Don't remind me!" Mary moaned. "Five more pages to go."

Yani leaned back in his chair to watch the show as Mary and Ettie immediately began bickering about Mary having to spend all night writing yet another essay. Ettie apparently needed her beauty sleep, and Mary's homework habits weren't helping.

He had another blind date to look forward to. Joy. Because the last four had gone so well. The best of all of Mary's blind dates had been Luke, and that was only because Luke was hot and he knew what he was doing between the sheets. Yani could appreciate that, but Luke hadn't been good boyfriend material. None of Mary's choices had been. Her friend Aaron who worked at a Christian Services organization sounded like a good guy, but Yani already had doubts that their beliefs and values would align closely enough to have something in common.

Yani would find out tomorrow afternoon. But before then, he had homework to make up for his late morning class. Mary and Ettie continued to bicker good-naturedly while Yani opened his computer and returned to his PowerPoint and the decision on which genocide he should study.

The café hadn't changed in the few months since Mary had last sent Yani there. The small booths and tables filling the space needed new upholstery and tabletops; the floor was cheap linoleum and the counters low-grade Formica. Despite all that, the coffee was always the best, and their muffins had won awards. It was the top college hangout in the area, but that didn't stop suits bringing their business meetings by or grannies having a little nosh for lunch.

Yani found a table in the corner and tossed the pink carnation Mary had pressed into his hand before he left onto the scarred surface. He only waited a couple of minutes before a young man about the same age as Yani walked into the shop. Yani wouldn't have noticed him if the man's eyes hadn't immediately focused on the flower.

Aaron was average-looking, but it wasn't a bad sort of average. He had light-brown hair and eyes, a straight nose, and full lips. He was thin and looked muscular, although that was hard to tell under the neat sweater and jeans he was wearing. Aaron wasn't overwhelmingly gorgeous like Luke, but Yani liked what he was seeing.

"I'm Aaron," Aaron said politely as he drew even with Yani's shoulder. "Mary told me to meet the person with the pink flower."

Yani turned and stood, only then realizing just how tall Aaron was. Craning his neck upward sent a little thrill through Yani's gut. He had a bit of a thing for taller men.

"I'm Yani…" Yani began, but trailed off when a stifled look of panic flashed across Aaron's face. Aaron's head whipped to the side so he could stare out the windows where an early autumn sunset was just beginning to color the sky over the city, and then turned back to carefully study Yani's face. "If you don't want to do this, I understand," Yani added quickly, hoping to prevent a panicked reaction. "I know Mary can be a little forceful about these things."

Aaron took a deep breath, visibly bracing himself before a smile lifted his lips just slightly.

"I'm sorry," he said, and the rich tone to his voice sent a shiver down Yani's spine—another positive check in Aaron's column. "It's just that you look like someone I know. Sit down and tell me your coffee order. I'll go get us drinks."

Yani asked for a French-vanilla coffee and watched as Aaron hurriedly turned around and headed to the counter. He pulled his phone out of his pocket, pressed a button, and began speaking intently into the phone while he waited in line. Yani sighed and leaned back in his seat. It was already all too obvious how the date was going to go. Aaron wasn't just uninterested—Yani was scaring him away. Maybe Aaron wasn't actually gay and Mary had tricked him into meeting Yani. That would certainly explain Aaron's surprise.

Aaron returned a few minutes later with a smile on his face and two coffees in hand. His phone had vanished again.

"Sorry about that," he said as he placed Yani's coffee onto the table. "I think we got off to a bad start. I'm Aaron and Mary told me to meet you here."

"I'm Yani," Yani answered slowly, wondering why he needed to repeat himself and skeptical of the sudden change of mood. "Mary said you work with her?"

"Ha-ha, yeah. She teaches girls that showing off their panties in too-short skirts isn't sexy while I try to tone down hormone-fueled aggression in boys who would be more than happy to see those panties. It's an adventure. Mary said you're a political-science major?"

Yani shook his head. "International relations. Same department, different area of study. I'm interested in international law."

"That's awesome," Aaron gaped, looking like he actually thought Yani was interesting. None of his shock and fear from before was evident anywhere in his face or voice. "I'm a student part-time in between all my jobs, but I've only been getting the basic requirements out of the way. I have no idea what I want to major in."

Magnified

Yani found that he was actually enjoying their conversation. Aaron was interesting, and his smile invited Yani to lean close as if their discussion was more personal than just basic introductions. He found his initial reticence from the awkward introduction fading away almost as quickly as Aaron's had. Yani couldn't help grinning widely at Aaron, glad to give him this second chance to enjoy their date.

"What jobs do you have?" Yani asked, genuinely curious.

Aaron shrugged. "This and that. You already know I work at Charlie's Hand, but I also do whatever odd jobs my family needs from me. Lately I've been cataloguing the library, which is huge."

"Your family has a huge library?" Yani asked. Was Aaron rich enough to live in a mansion that had enough space for a large library?

Aaron blushed, ducking his head slightly as he took a quick sip of his coffee. "Technically, it's not just my family's. We live in a very large apartment complex, and there's a library, pool, and playground. I'm making some extra cash by working there too."

"That's really cool," Yani couldn't help saying. He wished he had access to a pool and a library any time he wanted. Admittedly, he kind of did while living in the school dorms, since there was a pool and library available for his and any other student's use. He was just too lazy to take advantage when there were better things to do than swim and he had the internet to answer all of his academic questions.

The sun was fully set by seven fifteen, and Yani could feel his stomach growling. Since Aaron had bought the coffee, Yani sprang for a pair of chocolate-chip muffins that would hold them until dinner.

They continued to talk about inconsequential things as they ate, just to get to know each other a little better. Aaron was an only child, and his parents were divorced. He spent the summer with his mom in Worcester, but lived with his dad for the rest of the year despite being old enough to live on his own.

"They still fight over who gets to spend more time with me and why," Aaron explained with a wry smile. "It's easier to humor them for the moment, but once I have enough saved up, I'm getting my own place."

Yani couldn't help commiserating. "My parents want me to find a good job right out of college and start out on my own, yet at the same time they're not ready for me to leave the nest."

By seven forty-five, Yani started to get antsy that Luke might show up since the café was his favorite postclass hangout. Aaron, despite his attempts to continue their conversation, kept glancing out the windows where the moon was shining brightly over the skyscrapers. The Prudential Building was clearly outlined from where Yani was sitting.

He didn't want the date to end, though. He was having fun getting to know Aaron. There was real genuine warmth to him. He listened when Yani spoke as if what Yani had to say was interesting and didn't hesitate to add his own comments. It was probably the best first date Yani had ever had. However, after yet another long moment when Aaron's eyes strayed back outside, Yani gave up forcing the date to continue. There would be a second date, he hoped, where neither of them would be distracted. Yani started stacking the dishes together and stood so he could bring them to the return bin. Aaron got to his feet as well and waited by the table for Yani to return.

"I had fun," Aaron insisted when Yani stopped in front of him. "I would like to do this again I think."

He thought? Well, that wasn't particularly heartening to Yani's ears, yet he felt the same. He wanted to sit and chat with Aaron again, but only so long as Aaron didn't run off in a panic to jabber on his phone for a few minutes. A second date, this time without the awkward start, would be nice.

"I had fun too," Yani replied with a smile.

"How about next Tuesday at six?" Aaron's expression was earnest as his eyes searched Yani's face for the answer before Yani could open his mouth.

Yani would be getting back from traveling home for Yom Kippur just that morning, but it would be nice to have something to look forward to beyond catching up on more missed work.

"That sounds great," Yani said. "I'll see you then."

They awkwardly shook hands because a hug was too intimate for a first date and Yani didn't want to move too quickly, and Yani led the way out of the café. Yani took a right turn to head back to his dorm, and Aaron turned left toward the nearest T stop.

Mary hadn't done such a poor job setting up his blind date this time, Yani thought as he bent his nose underneath the collar of his jacket. The wind off the ocean had a bite to it, despite it still only being September, and he quickened his steps through the browning leaves dotting the sidewalk.

Aaron was handsome but not overpoweringly pretty, something Yani definitely appreciated after Luke's almost overwhelming beauty. Yes, the date had been awkward quite a few times and not just due to first-date jitters. Aaron had been preoccupied with something else—that was clear. Yet when Yani had gotten Aaron to focus on their conversation, he had been funny and warm. There was potential between them for their first date to become so much more. Yani could only hope Aaron would resolve whatever had been bothering him by the time their second date came around. It was certainly something to look forward to, Yani thought with a smile.

He just couldn't tell Mary about that thought or she would gloat forever.

Yani rounded a corner, the buildings of his school's dorms just ahead, when someone stepped up next to him. Yani turned his head to see why someone was interfering with his personal space. He never heard the second person come up behind him, but when his eyes met with the furious glare of the too-close man, he gasped just as a strange-smelling cloth was clapped over his face.

The world swam in his vision for a long moment, only the glaring blue eyes still staring at him clear in the nighttime air. Then everything went black.

Yani blinked a few times, trying to clear the fuzziness from his mind, which whirled with scattered thoughts like little tadpoles stuck in a bucket. He didn't dare shake his head as that would only make things worse.

Slowly, the world around him began to come into focus. He was in a large room, empty save for himself, with a hard-packed dirt floor and white walls. The space was circular, and as Yani turned his head he saw the outline of a door that lacked a handle on his side and a series of small windows no more than a hand-span wide at approximately eye level.

Yani tried to turn around to get a better look at the door, but the clank of heavy metal made him freeze in place. His body felt weighted, but he had assumed that was only residual from the drug. A glance at his wrists and ankles showed otherwise. Thick, silver manacles were wrapped around his limbs, dragging his body down until his knees were hidden in a pile of gray, heavy, dusty matter. The chains also vanished beneath the waist-high material.

Magnified

And it hit Yani. He had been kidnapped and chained in some strange place.

His breathing quickened, his heart pounded, and he let out little yips of panic as his fingers scrabbled around the manacle holding his left wrist in place. He couldn't find a keyhole or a hinge, just the large ring that connected the manacle to the chain. His fingers curled involuntarily around the chain, and he pulled as hard and frantically as he could. Clouds of the dust erupted in the air as he gasped and sobbed and yanked to no avail. The chains were clearly hooked to something underneath the dust, but the panic in Yani's head wouldn't allow that rational thought to take full form. He continued to pull, certain that his next yank would loosen something, certain that the blood staining his wrist where the manacle was cutting into his skin was inconsequential to the necessity of just pulling a little harder. He had to get free. He had to because being locked up like this wasn't okay. It wasn't.

"Vampire," a voice crackled through a loudspeaker. Yani let out a little scream of surprise at the sudden noise and managed to painfully whack his thigh with the length of chain he dropped in reaction. "Your species has been judged and found wanting; your punishment decided."

"I told you I met him in daylight," a second, familiar voice interrupted what sounded like a practiced speech.

"Quiet, Aaron. Your foolishness is unneeded at this point," the first voice snapped, sounding muffled as if he had pulled away from the microphone for a brief moment. His voice returned to full strength a second later. "Vampire, you shall die as all of your kind must. Return to the hell from whence you came."

The crackle of the loudspeaker faded away, replaced by a loud, metallic groan. Yani looked up when the ceiling began to retract. The first hints of daylight began to curl along one rounded wall, the beam quickly widening as the spotlights that had previously lit the room winked out one by one. The sunlight inched closer, as if his doom were ponderously taking one step at a time, the executioner's heavy axe held threateningly over one shoulder.

The sun hit his legs first, where he was still partially submerged beneath the pile of dirt. The light crept up his feet, past his knees and hips, until his torso was outlined in the sun. He had to lift one hand to shield his eyes as the sunlight shone directly at his face.

His hand was covered in grime, the blood from his wrist dripping slowly down to stain it from an odd gray color to a murky red. His first thought was, *Oh god, how long have I been asleep?* His second thought exploded slowly through his mind, like watching a bomb on a TV news show in slow motion.

They had called him a vampire and told him he was about to die. Then they'd opened the roof and let the sun shine down. All mythology suggested that when exposed to the sun, vampires exploded into flames and their bodies became dust. Oh, god. He was sitting in the destroyed bodies of dead vampires. He wasn't sitting in dirt; he was sitting in ashes. Yani was chained up in a graveyard!

No. He was chained in an execution ground.

Yani fought to stay calm. The chains weren't long enough to allow him to move away from the mound of ashes. There was nothing he could do to leave. Besides, he hadn't burst into flames like the vampires. Surely they would come to investigate soon and would let him go when they realized he was human. They had to.

Time slowly passed, the angle of the sun against the walls changing minutely throughout the day. Yani fought to keep from hyperventilating, trying to keep his mind blank so panic didn't reassert itself. His wrist was still bleeding sluggishly;

every time it started to scab, it itched and Yani involuntarily scratched it back open.

He couldn't help wondering if the vampires he was sitting in had met the sun cowering or with their fangs bared defiantly. Had they struggled as Yani had, fighting with the chains and their fear, or had their resistance died when their inevitable death became clear? Yani felt sad for them, but he hoped they had lived many full lifetimes before being so cruelly captured and dispatched.

Yani looked at his legs, still buried underneath the dust, at the sheer amount of vampire ashes that surrounded him, and shuddered. "*Baruch dayan emet* (Blessed is the True Judge)," he whispered reflexively. It was the Jewish blessing for death, not in mourning, but rather to provide comfort to those who mourned. Only god knew the reasons why a person died. (S)he judged a person and saw the truth of them, and chose who would live and who would die. All Yani could do was trust that god knew what was right in the case of the poor vampires surrounding him.

The day continued to slowly pass. Every once in a while, he heard someone squabbling behind the lone door. Eyes would peek out through the windows, shocked to see his still-living self. The third time that happened, Yani broke and called out.

"I have to pee," he yelled loudly at the two pairs of eyes staring at him. "Can you please take me to the bathroom?"

There was another muffled discussion behind the door, and the eyes vanished from sight. A loud creak echoed through the room as the door slowly opened. It was thick metal and heavy, judging by the effort Aaron used to push the door. Aaron was glaring over his shoulder at someone Yani couldn't see.

"I told you he's not a vampire. He just looks like one of the ones in the archive," Aaron snapped. Once the door was finally propped open all the way, he let go and hurried toward Yani. He sank to his knees in the ashes at Yani's side and reached out to take Yani's hands. He mumbled something too low for Yani to catch, and the manacles fell open with a clack. Aaron dug into the ashes to find Yani's ankles next, the metal falling away after another mumble.

Aaron helped Yani stand, his limbs awkward and unwieldy from his day spent immobile. While Yani tried to find his balance, Aaron roughly brushed the ashes from Yani's clothes. He reopened the cut on Yani's wrist by accident and gasped when he saw the blood.

"Let me show you to the bathroom and then get you a clean Band-Aid," Aaron insisted. He gripped Yani's elbow to steady him and led the way back through the open door.

There was a waiting crowd on the other side. Men and women alike had their backs pressed against the walls as Yani shakily clung to Aaron's arm. Most were just glaring hatefully at him, but a couple were openly carrying guns. One man even had a cocked crossbow pointed at the ground. The fierce glare in his eyes told Yani he could and would aim and shoot in a matter of milliseconds.

Aaron led the way into a hallway on the other side of the room where a unisex-bathroom sign hung on the wall next to a nondescript doorway. The hall was painted white and there were more doors farther down, but Yani only had eyes for that sign. He hadn't been lying about needing to pee. It had been hours and his bladder was aching.

Aaron pushed the door open, but Yani let go of his arm and stepped forward on his own. He didn't need help peeing, although he didn't need a crowd watching him either. Aaron was followed into the bathroom by two men as Yani slipped into the lone stall, unzipped, and aimed at the waiting toilet.

"He was bleeding. Did you see that?" a man's voice asked, sounding incredulous.

"I did!" a woman's voice answered. "Means he still has a heartbeat! And I didn't see any silver burns from the manacles."

"He isn't burned from sun exposure either. There's obviously something else going on here," the first man agreed with a sigh.

Yani finished and flushed, zipping his pants back up before leaving the stall and making a beeline for the sink. He scrubbed his hands, trying to get as much of the dust off as he could. He used soap twice, the second time hissing in pain as he cleaned his cut too and it stung. He splashed water on his face when his hands were clean and then groped for a paper towel to dry off.

His image in the mirror told him he was as clean as he would get without a full shower. It also told him why he had been mistaken for a vampire. He was the mirror image of Uncle Yakov, after all.

"Let's get you bandaged up," Aaron said.

Yani nodded and pushed away from the sink. Aaron held out a clean paper towel that he had folded neatly. Yani took it and pressed it against his wrist and followed Aaron out of the bathroom and farther down the hallway. Their audience trailed behind.

Aaron led the way to a small sitting room a bit farther down the hall. There were two large couches around a low table. The sidebar along the wall held glasses, but no water or food. Now that the most pressing issue had been taken care of, the fact that Yani was thirsty and hungry was quickly becoming all he could think of. His stomach let out a growl, which made one of the men watching flinch.

"We still have some sandwiches left from lunch, right?" Aaron asked. Yani sank onto one of the couches, grateful to have something soft to sit on again. The man who had flinched hurried off.

Aaron sank onto the second couch with a groan. He rubbed his forehead with one hand before placing both hands into his lap and looking over at Yani.

"You have no idea how sorry I am about all this, Yani," he tried to explain, looking earnest and contrite. Yani didn't know how to answer. He didn't quite know how he felt about everything that had happened. He was actually feeling rather numb and hungry. Thinking wasn't high on his list of priorities at the moment. "You look almost exactly like an old photograph of a vampire I literally just finished filing in the library before I met you on our date. I called my dad to double-check, and next thing I know your unconscious body is being locked up in that horrible room."

"What is this place?"

Aaron snorted, his lip curling slightly in disgust. "It's a hunters' compound. Anything they think of as a threat to humanity they hunt and destroy. Vampires are a priority, so when I called in to verify whether vampires could go out in daylight because I might be sitting across from one at a café, they went a bit nuts. I am so very sorry. I've told my father so many times to cool it with his hunter crap around me. I had to grow up with it, but all I'm willing to do to help them is get paid to organize their library."

"You have so little respect for the good work we do," another voice snapped. Yani couldn't stop a flinch as the man with the voice from the loudspeaker stomped into view. He hovered menacingly over Yani, one hand on his holstered gun and the other holding a piece of paper.

"Your work is bull," Aaron snapped back. "You hunt creatures that haven't done any harm just because you're afraid of them, and you go so overboard that you've traumatized Yani!"

"Your ignorance will cost you one day."

Magnified

Yani looked back and forth between the two men, noting the similarities. The second man must have been Aaron's father. They shared the same eyes and nose, but where on the father it looked harsh, on Aaron, with the much more delicate features he must have gotten from his mother, he looked young and handsome.

"So only one of you is a mass murderer?" Yani asked, wondering afterward why his voice sounded so matter-of-fact when one of the men who so callously disregarded his life was glaring at him as if he were some sort of disgusting bug.

"Tell me who this man is," Aaron's father snarled, dropping the piece of paper he still held and blithely ignoring Yani's comment.

Yani looked down at the photo and shook his head slowly. It felt like there were cobwebs where his brain used to be, but even he could recognize his own face in the grainy black-and-white photograph that had been photocopied onto the paper. The shape of the eyebrows was different; Yani had Dad's eyebrows, but the rest of him was entirely from Mom's side of the family. His hair had the same curls and his lips the same bow. They could have been identical twins, Yakov and Yani. There was no way Yani was going to tell anyone here that fact, of course.

"It's difficult to explain," Yani slowly replied.

The man who had gone for food returned before Yani could continue or Aaron's father's angry growl could get any louder. He set a plate with a piled-high sandwich and an unopened bottle of water down in front of Yani.

Yani's stomach let out an audible growl, louder even than Aaron's father's, but Yani could tell there were things on the sandwich he couldn't eat. He was starving, yes, and beggars shouldn't be choosers, but he wasn't about to die if he didn't eat right at that moment. Yani pulled the top bun off the sandwich and removed three slices of bacon and two slices of cheese. He left the turkey and roast beef alone, returned the bun, and finally took a gigantic bite.

The sandwich tasted funny. The disgusting flavor of bacon made his already rolling stomach feel nauseous, but the rest of the meat was tasty. Yani opened the water and gulped down as much as he could to wash away the bad taste in his mouth from the dust and the bacon before returning to his food.

"Tell me," Aaron's father hissed, one finger pointing at the photo.

Yani swallowed, gulped a few more mouthfuls of water, and turned back to the picture.

"Back in Poland, I had a huge family. My great-grandmother Chana had her siblings and those siblings had kids of their own. Then they were deported to different ghettos and concentration camps. Gramma never saw her siblings again. The only family we can say for certain survived the Germans were Gramma Chana and her four children she brought with her to America. We never found the rest of the family. I'd be interested to know where you got this photo," Yani continued, feeling much better with food and water in his stomach. His brain was really starting to kick in, and the story he was fabricating was a stroke of genius he hadn't thought himself capable of just yet. "It could lead us to some long-lost family."

Aaron's father snorted in disgust and yanked the paper off the table before turning on one heel and stomping out of the room as abruptly as he had entered.

"Get him out of here," he snapped in the doorway, not breaking stride to look back.

Yani finished his sandwich and water before turning to look at Aaron. Aaron was wringing his hands together in his lap. He looked lost and hurt, but Yani didn't have any sympathy. Aaron might not adhere to his father's beliefs, but he wasn't doing anything to stop him either.

"I'm sorry, Yani," he repeated, slowly lifting his anguished eyes to look directly at Yani. "I hope you can forgive me for letting this happen."

Yani shook his head. He wasn't thinking about any of that at the moment. Maybe when he was feeling totally coherent, he would yell at Mary for setting him up with another whacko, but Yani needed space and time to think everything through and to come to terms with the world he had been so ruthlessly exposed to. Only then could he decide if forgiving Aaron for being a part of genocide was possible.

"I think we should cancel our date next Tuesday," Yani finally replied. "I can't be around you right now."

"Okay," Aaron sighed. "Okay. I understand. Manny, will you drive Yani back to his dorm?"

The man who had brought Yani the sandwich flinched and turned his head to stare incredulously at Yani.

"Is that safe?" he asked breathlessly.

Yani groaned as he levered himself to his feet. "Yes, it's safe. I'm just a regular human. Although it would be nice if someone found my phone and wallet before I left."

Manny nodded his head jerkily. "I'll find them." He hurried from the room, leaving Aaron to guide the way back into the bland hallway and through another nondescript door that led to a large underground garage. Manny arrived a few minutes later carrying a small plastic bag with Yani's belongings in it. He indicated a car nearby, and Yani climbed into the passenger seat.

He didn't say goodbye to Aaron as the car pulled away. Yani actually hoped he never had to see Aaron again. The car stopped at the end of the driveway, and Manny held out a blindfold toward Yani.

"Don't know what you are, but we can't have you going to the police over this and bringing them back here." Manny was holding his hand rigidly as if he was trying to keep himself from shaking even as he tried to be stern with Yani.

"What would I tell them? That you locked me in a room full of vampire dust?" Yani sighed, wishing this was over already, but he took the blindfold and tied it over his eyes. He couldn't see anything with the blindfold on. Manny must have done something to double-check because a moment later he let out a satisfied grunt and the car started moving forward again.

They drove for a while, probably going in circles to throw Yani off. He was too tired to bother with counting lefts and rights and all that nonsense. He instead sat quietly, hoping they really would take him back to his dorm eventually.

"You can take it off," Manny said after at least a half hour.

They were not too far outside Boston Yani saw as he blinked while his eyes adjusted to the sunlight. Yani could see the Citgo sign just ahead. After a short time on the highway, Manny pulled off into crazy Boston street traffic. He double-parked at the curb to let Yani out when they reached his dorm. Yani didn't say anything as he got out of the car and slammed the door behind him. He let himself into the dorm building with his pass card and trudged up the stairs to his room.

His roommate, Brandon, was out for the day, which was a relief. Yani dropped his things on the bed, grabbed his shower kit, and headed for the communal bathrooms at a jog. The hot water and soap felt divine. Getting himself clean was even more therapeutic than food had been.

Magnified

Water in the dorms only ran cold when every shower was in use at the same time, which wasn't the case at this time of the day. Yani didn't know how long he stood there, but his fingers were wrinkled and aching with heat by the time he finally reached out to shut the water off. He used his towel to dry himself and then wrapped it around his waist for the trip back to his room.

Yani pulled on fresh boxers and a pair of sweatpants and then went over to his desk and opened his computer. His email pinged almost immediately, but he flipped through the browser windows until his half-finished letter to Uncle Yakov popped up. He wrote a few more sentences, hit Print, and found an envelope. The address was still saved in his phone, so Yani sealed his letter, found a sweatshirt, and headed downstairs to the mailroom. It didn't matter how much the stamps overseas cost, because Yakov needed to read the letter.

Afterwards, Yani trudged back to his room, curled up in his bed, and yanked his covers over his head. His brain shut back down with welcome relief, and real sleep took him away.

Dear Uncle Yakov and Uncle Martin,

This past Rosh Hashanah I stole your mailing address from my mother. She was entrusted with it when Great-grandmother Chana died. I don't think Mom's been writing to you, but I thought you might enjoy knowing how the family is doing. I guess I'll start with me, since I'm writing the letter. I will get to Gramma Chana next, and Uncle Shimon too, don't worry.

My name is Yani Goldhaber. My mom is Grandpa Gideon's third child. You and I met at Gramma Chana's funeral.

Mell Eight

That was what I was going to write, but everything's changed. I was just accosted by a group of vampire hunters. They thought I was you, Uncle Yakov, because we look so much alike. They have a picture of you, and maybe also a picture of Uncle Martin. Please be careful and stay away from Boston if you're planning to do any traveling.

Sincerely,

Yani Goldhaber

"What do you think, darling?" Martin asked, looking over his shoulder where Yakov had been reading the strange letter they had just received in the mail. "Shall we go visit your family?"

Yakov snarled something impolite under his breath in Yiddish, which made Martin smile as it always did, and ran a hand through his hair. "If they're going to be harassing my family, then yes. We need to nip this in the bud before it gets any worse."

Martin smiled and tilted his head back to take a swift kiss. There were many reasons he had fallen in love with Yakov, but seeing him with his family, holding his baby boy to his chest or playing in front of the fire at night—not that dear Chana had known Martin was nearby at the time—had cemented Martin's feelings.

"Yani must be the kid we spoke with at Chana's funeral," Yakov mused, resting his chin on Martin's shoulder once their kiss ended. "He must be in his midtwenties now, I think. Just the perfect age to look like a vampire trapped in time."

"Particularly if this group of hunters somehow captured a photograph of you, darling," Martin sighed in agreement. "That child we met did look surprisingly similar to you.

This hunter organization might prove to be larger and more dangerous than I originally surmised. Let me make some phone calls to some friends, and then I shall arrange our travel. Sometime after Yom Kippur, I presume?"

"Thank you, Martin," Yakov said. He nuzzled his nose into Martin's neck, a loving gesture because his sharp teeth didn't bite down.

"I know, darling. I love you too."

Two: Atonement

In English, Yom Kippur meant Day of Atonement. It was a day when Jews around the world asked for forgiveness of their sins over the past year in the hope that god would inscribe their names in the book of life for the coming year. It was also a day of reflection, to look back on life and see what could be improved or done better in the year ahead.

Yani was certainly reflecting, but he somehow didn't think that reflecting on vampires was exactly what god had intended for his time in synagogue. He stood when the rabbi indicated the congregation should stand and bowed or beat his chest with a fist in sorrow when the prayers indicated he was supposed to, but the words coming out of his mouth didn't have any meaning to his brain. It was all rote memorization from past Yom Kippur services.

There wasn't anything he could do about the dead vampires. There must have been dozens of them, given the sheer amount of ashes Yani had been sitting in. He had even done what he could to save any future vampire victims by alerting Uncle Yakov that there was a problem in Boston. Presumably, word had gone out to the vampires in New England to stay away from Boston until the hunters moved on.

It wasn't that Yani was still caught up in his own kidnapping. Yes, it had been horrifying, but he hadn't been harmed. They had let him go after nothing more than a scare. He did have nightmares about screaming vampires as the sun began to peek through the retracting roof. Sometimes those vampires had Yani's face, although whether he was seeing himself or Yakov was questionable. But the cut on his arm had healed without a scar, and the memories were beginning to blunt with age. He hoped that in a few more weeks even the nightmares would stop.

None of that would save the vampires the hunters were killing.

Okay, the truth was, Yani didn't know anything about the vampires in question. He had looked online for information about vampires, but every single website said something different and often contradicted what the previous one had told him. The mythology differed by region of the world, religious belief system, and even various popular authors' descriptions. All Yani had to go on was the dust and the little Gramma had told him. It was entirely possible that vampires were evil. Perhaps they killed for their blood or terrorized their victims for fun, but equally, Yani wondered how many were just innocently going about their lives and were discovered and killed by the hunters for no reason other than they existed. It was that latter idea that made Yani feel twitchy. He needed to know more about vampires before he could give an honest opinion.

Heck, even if the vampires were committing murders every night they didn't deserve immediate and terrifying execution.

Magnified

That was his political-science background kicking in from the semester on dictatorships and absolute power. The ability to arbitrarily decide who lived and died based on a personal set of beliefs and morals inevitably led to intense corruption and eventual retribution. Without safeguards like the rule of law or a proper court system, innocent vampires would have been condemned for the same reason as guilty ones, and at some point in the near future that would come back to bite the hunters.

Services hadn't yet ended when Mom and Dad decided to leave. Yom Kippur was an all-day event, but most Conservative Jews came for the morning and evening portions of the service and stayed home for the rest of it. It was only one o'clock, and Yani's stomach was already growling with hunger. Mom was starting to get snappish, as she always did when she hadn't eaten in a long while. Shira had a full-on pout going in the back seat of the car.

She wasn't old enough according to Jewish law to participate in the twenty-four-hour fast of atonement. Only Jewish adults, those post-b'nai mitzvah, were expected to fast. Shira, though, was considered old enough to take care of herself. Mom and Dad weren't going to have to make her lunch, because she could reach the bread and use the toaster without help. Or Shira could fast too. Yani had when he was eleven, but at the time it had been because he felt he had something to prove. He was a big kid and could do it! Shira had never fallen under that fallacy, but she was still young enough to have wanted a full breakfast of eggs and bagels—instead of the rushed Pop-Tart—and a tuna-and-cheese sandwich with all the trimmings for lunch.

Heck, Yani could use a tuna sandwich. It would shut his rumbling stomach up, but that wasn't the spirit of the holiday. Yom Kippur was about asking for forgiveness and showing his sorrow for the mistakes he had made over the past year through fasting and repentant prayer.

Mell Eight

The sky was gray and cloudy outside from a storm that stretched from Tennessee through Maine, drenching every state in between. The bus ride home had been damp too, but luckily the rain held off as the car pulled onto their driveway. Dad parked in the garage, and they all trooped out.

It was naptime. That was what Jews did on Yom Kippur when they weren't in synagogue. They napped. A schluffy. It made the time pass without constant awareness of the hole ominously growing in the stomach. Yani hurried upstairs to his room to change into much more comfortable jeans and a shirt, dumping his jacket and tie on his desk chair because he would have to put them back on later for the afternoon service. He grabbed his computer and crawled into bed.

Maybe he would take a nap, but since he was hungry it felt like the perfect opportunity to start researching the Ukrainian famine, caused by Soviet Communist zealousness, that had eventually killed millions of people. He was going to compare and contrast it to the Chinese famine two decades later that had also killed millions in the name of the might of Communism. It was an interesting topic, considering the influence of Communism that had caused the famines to occur and had kept the rest of the democratic world ignorant.

Yani worked for the rest of the afternoon, digging up websites and trying to find research on Google Books. It was harder than it looked, since the governments that had so eagerly covered up the entire debacle were only slowly releasing information about the famines. He consulted the textbook for the class more often than anything.

Dad always passed out on the couch downstairs in the family room, newspaper in hand as he snored lightly. Mom slept in their bedroom down the hall. Yani didn't keep track of what Shira did, but he suspected she had squirreled herself down in the basement with a bag of chips to watch cartoons in the rec room. When Yani heard water running from his parents' room and footsteps on the landing, he knew it was time to save his work and start getting changed. There was one more service at synagogue, and then it was off to Aunt Miriam's house for Break Fast.

All of the kids in the synagogue were invited up to the bimah with their shofars as the service drew to a close. There were already people inching out of their seats, their eyes firmly focused on the extra-large platters of sliced challah tantalizingly waiting in the back of the sanctuary.

The final prayer was read, and the great blat of two dozen shofars, including a few plastic ones for the youngest kids who couldn't pucker their lips properly to make the ram's horn shofar sound, signaled the end of the holiday. Shira was on the bimah pretending she knew how to actually blow the family's shofar along with all of Yani's younger cousins. Yani was quick to follow his parents to the back of the room where he joined in with all the other adults in stuffing his face.

The challah could have been the stalest, most vile-tasting challah ever baked, but Yani wouldn't have noticed. It tasted sweet and filling with every bite. He grabbed a plastic cup of apple juice off a nearby tray—the first drink he had been allowed to have all day—and downed that too.

With his initial hunger sated, Yani stepped aside to allow others a chance to eat. Auntie Miriam had bagels and lox, quiche, and blintz soufflé, as well as a plethora of desserts waiting for them. The faster they could collect Shira and get to the car, the sooner they would have real food to shovel in their stomachs.

Yani popped his last bite of challah into his mouth as he followed Mom and Dad to the coatroom. The fleeting thought that it was nice that the bread didn't have the revolting bitterness of a bacon aftertaste flittered through his mind, but Yani quickly suppressed it. Instead he yanked his nice autumn coat off the hanger and jammed his arms into the sleeves. Shira was whining about having to leave all her friends so soon—never mind that all of her friends were being hustled out the door to their own family's Break Fasts—and Dad was busy trying not to lose his hunger-strained temper at her whining.

Finally, they all managed to get in the car and they were off.

Normal family events consisted of hellos and hugs at the door, general chatting until everyone arrived, and then a polite sit-down dinner. All those rules of propriety were thrown out the window for Break Fast. After a full twenty-four hours of no food and no water, people hurried into Auntie Miriam's house, tossed their coats onto a nearby couch, grabbed a plate, and started stuffing their faces while standing around the overfilled table. Small talk didn't start until after the first bagel was just a happy memory, and even then, people usually went for their second helpings of everything instead.

Yani was no exception. His first plate was a large onion bagel slathered with cream cheese and topped with lox and fresh-cut red onion. His second plate was a piece of challah drowned in tuna salad and swiss cheese with a hard-boiled egg and some quiche and soufflé on the side. By the time he was finally stuffed, the pies and cakes on the dessert table had been decimated and he was ready for a food-coma nap.

It was getting late too. Shira and Mom and Dad had missed school and work for the weekday holiday. Despite the fact that Yom Kippur fell on the same day every year, it did so on the Hebrew lunar calendar, and that didn't always match up with the Western solar one. Shira and Mom and Dad had to get up early in the morning for work, and Yani had a bus to catch.

They said their goodbyes, everyone hugging carefully around the food-babies in their stomachs, and then headed home. Shira went to bed, and Yani headed upstairs to his room to pack for his early bus. Dad was going to drop Yani off before he headed to work, and Yani was hoping to get back to Boston in time for his afternoon classes.

His genocide and human rights professor wanted a prospectus and a thesis statement for the essay Yani had been working on. They were presenting it in class for feedback, and Yani didn't want to miss that opportunity.

He changed into pajamas once his suitcase was packed and climbed into bed. His eyes slid shut slowly. Yani hoped that this time he didn't wake up thrashing because the covers reminded his dreaming mind of being buried in dust.

"You're missing the geopolitical aspects," his professor admonished when Yani finished explaining what his essay was going to be about. She held out her hand for the paper Yani had been reading from, and he handed it over to her. "What was the US doing and what preoccupied Europe that allowed both genocides to occur unimpeded? Why were they so reluctant to interfere with the Communist world?"

Yani nodded, hoping he looked thoughtful instead of letting on that he was inwardly cursing himself. He had written up a quick prospectus and thesis statement on the bus ride back to Boston, but had totally forgotten the second half of the paper. It wasn't just a paper about the genocides themselves; it was about the politics of the world at the time as well. He would need to compare and contrast that for both genocides too. His paper had basically just doubled in workload, but luckily he still had two months to get it together.

Yani returned to his seat, and the next student stood and walked to the front of the room to present their idea. The clock on the wall slowly ticked away as the presentations ended and the professor began her lecture for the day. They were covering Rwanda, starting from the country itself and finishing with the failure of the international community to act. It was interesting material, but Yani was glad when the clock finally indicated that class time was over. He hadn't unpacked yet, and Mary was expecting him to have dinner with her in a half hour. Yani saved his class notes and tucked his computer into his backpack.

"Your presentation was definitely the most interesting," Rachel said slickly as she sidled up to Yani's side. She was wearing a low-cut blouse, which was probably supposed to be worn with a layered shirt underneath, and tight jeans. She was bending over slightly at Yani's side, giving him an uninterrupted view of her lacy pink bra, and looking up at him through her overly darkened lashes.

"Thank you, Rachel," Yani said shortly, hoping he could escape while knowing he was in heaps of trouble. Rachel was a leech, and apparently he was now her newest victim.

She giggled, the sound grating on Yani's ears as he tried to gently muscle past her and head toward the classroom door. "Oh, call me Chava. It's my Hebrew name, you know." She was hurrying to keep up with him while still fluttering her lashes and trying to make her boobs bounce invitingly. She had so chosen the wrong target. She was pretty, sure, but besides the fact he was gay, he didn't like the way she crossed every personal space boundary. She made him feel really uncomfortable.

Yani kept walking, not even acknowledging Rachel was still bouncing along at his side, giggling and flashing her skinny-jean clad butt as she hurried in front of him to grab the door. They walked out into the quad side by side, and Yani immediately turned toward his dorm.

"Are you going to be at dinner later?" Rachel asked, one hand reaching out to grab Yani's arm to keep him from wandering off. Luckily, she was heading in the other direction.

Magnified

Yani looked down at the overly long nails painted with bright flowers and shrugged, both in answer and to get her hand off him. Her touch made his skin crawl. Yani didn't know why, because he had no problem with Mary or any of his other friends touching him, but something about Rachel was seriously rubbing him the wrong way.

"See you later, Rachel," Yani said politely and kept walking, hoping that would be enough to get her to leave.

Once he was sure Rachel wasn't following him any longer, Yani pulled out his phone and texted Mary. *Rachel's chosen me as her next victim*, he wrote while holding back a sigh. Mary replied with a smiley face with its tongue sticking out.

Yani swiped his campus card across the card reader. It beeped and the door clicked as it unlocked. He walked inside, took the stairs up to the third floor, and turned left to get to his room. His key card unlocked the door, and Yani hurried inside.

The dorm housed students from all four years, but the nicer rooms were always picked off by the upperclassmen before the freshmen had a chance. The room Yani shared with Brandon was big; they didn't have to worry about their stuff getting mixed up like the underclassmen did. Mary and Ettie lived in a suite in the dorm next door, which meant they shared a large room and two other people shared a second large room connected via a spacious common room.

Brandon had class until eight that night, so Yani had the room to himself as he dug his computer out of his bag and dropped it on his bed next to his suitcase. He unzipped the duffel bag and started putting his clothes away. There was nothing quite like doing laundry at home to remind him why he hated the machines in the dorm basement.

By the time he was done cleaning, Yani's stomach was rumbling. He tucked the empty bag underneath his bed, gathered his campus card, and headed back out. The trek to the nearby dining hall only took a few minutes. The smell of food and the noise of fellow students chatting and eating met him as he opened the door and stepped inside. He swiped his card for his meal plan and headed straight for the trays.

"Over here!" Mary called, waving one hand from across the room where she, Ettie, and Tony had taken over a large table in the corner.

Yani waved back to let Mary know he had seen her and instead turned toward the waiting buffet of food. He filled a tray with the chicken and pasta being offered and headed over to the salad bar to assuage the guilt he was still feeling over that second slice of pie the night before.

"Hey, Yani," Rachel gushed as she dropped her tray onto the counter next to him. She reached for the lettuce tongs just out of easy grasp, which allowed her to bend over to show Yani she had changed her shirt and a bra wasn't part of the current ensemble. "You want to come over to my apartment later? I need a little help with my thesis statement." She batted her false lashes at him and wiggled her chest. Yani quickly turned his eyes away before Rachel's over-the-top act made him even more uncomfortable than it already had. He put some carrots on his plate.

"No thank you, Rachel. I'm gay and not interested," Yani said firmly, but politely. He picked up his tray and made to leave, only to be stopped when Rachel placed one hand on Yani's chest.

"I told you," she simpered in what she probably thought was a sexy bedroom voice. "Call me Chava. Why don't you come eat with me and we can…discuss," she emphasized with a sly lick of her very-red-painted lips, "my paper."

"Sorry, Rachel," Yani insisted, stepping back and to the side to escape her. "I already have a seat saved, and if you're having trouble with your paper, then you should speak with the professor."

He hurried away before Rachel could follow, stopping quickly at the drink station to fill a cup of juice, and plopped down in the empty seat next to Tony a few seconds later.

Tony was smirking, and Mary was giggling into her chocolate milk. For a second, Yani thought Ettie had missed the confrontation before she looked up from her burger and lifted one sardonic and pierced eyebrow.

"Someone save me," Yani gasped dramatically, one hand going to his forehead in a fake swoon. "Rachel's what? A junior? How did she ever make it through freshman year?"

Tony snorted. "By sleeping with all of her male professors and sleeping with anyone intelligent who could be duped into writing her papers for her, duh."

"What's she calling herself this time?" Mary asked, her grin unabated. "When she was going after that Evangelical Christian boy in her psych class last semester, she called herself Mary, after Mary Magdalene." Mary rolled her eyes, even though that was the same reason her parents had named her Mary.

"Chava," Yani said. "She said that's her Hebrew name." Instead of changing Rachel to Rakhel, which would have made sense, she had come out of left field with Chava. Not that she was even Jewish.

Mary snorted with more laughter. "Well, her gaydar is broken, that's for sure. Don't let her get to you."

Tony nodded in agreement, and they all fell silent for a few minutes as they ate. Tony's full name was Mercutio. He went by Tony for his own sanity and because he respected his Hispanic heritage. His mother was a flower child, despite the fact that it had gone out of style decades ago. In one of her pot-induced hazes, she had met a drifter out of Mexico, and Tony was the result. He had typical Latino good looks, with high cheekbones and tanned skin. From his mother, he had gotten blue eyes and a pert nose. He needed to cut his hair a little shorter, but aside from that Tony was really very handsome. Yani had been interested in Tony for a bit, until he realized Tony had a high-school sweetheart that he was still seeing. He had been a close friend ever since.

They finished their meals, and manfully, Yani didn't join Ettie as she went on a quest to the dessert buffet. That second piece of pie, and the brownie, and the slice of cheesecake were still on his mind.

"Aaron wants to see you again," Mary said gently when a lull in their conversation about homework didn't lead to another topic. Yani hadn't told her exactly what had happened to make the date go so badly. How could he have explained vampires and hunters to her? Mary had been able to glean through speaking with Yani and Aaron on her own that things hadn't gone well.

Yani shook his head in denial, his good mood broken with the reminder of the horrific things he had seen. His healed wrist throbbed in memory, but he pushed it aside as forcefully as he could.

"He just wants to apologize again for whatever he did," Mary insisted. "Please, Yani, he's my friend, too, and I can tell he feels really bad about it."

Yani didn't know how to answer. He didn't really have a reason to say no aside from the fact he didn't want to be reminded of being chained in that room of death. Yet he didn't really want to say yes either. The date itself had been awkward, but Yani now knew Aaron had only acted odd because Yani looked like a vampire. Once Yani took that issue out of the equation, it honestly was one of the nicest dates he'd had in a long time. Hell, even if Yani included those stilted moments, it was still a good first date. What had occurred afterward had

Yani hesitating, although even that wasn't Aaron's fault. Aaron had fought with his father so they would let Yani go.

"Tomorrow night," Mary insisted. "You only have that math class in the morning with me. Aaron's got a double lecture until eight, but he wants to meet you after. The café at eight fifteen."

Mary didn't bother getting Yani's agreement. She knew better, instead leaving it open-ended for Yani to decide. The guilt of not giving Aaron a chance to really apologize and explain himself would force Yani into going before long, which Mary knew, but she also didn't want to pressure him into a bad situation. If he were truly uncomfortable, he could stay home, but Yani had already started thinking about which reading assignments he should get done tonight rather than tomorrow night, since he was apparently going to be busy.

Mary resolutely turned to Tony to ask him about his girlfriend, and Yani gladly turned his focus to that.

The café hadn't changed in the few days since Yani had last sat at the corner table with Aaron. He didn't know why he'd thought the place should have transformed, or why he hesitated before walking in. It hadn't been the café that had scarred him for life, but somehow the association was still there.

Aaron was already there, his hands wrapped around a steaming cup of coffee. His back was to the door, which gave Yani plenty of time to study Aaron's slumped shoulders and lowered head. He wasn't drinking from his coffee; rather, the steam was bathing his face in apparent comfort.

Yani was only five minutes late, but Aaron looked like he would be willing to sit in his chair for hours while his coffee cooled and Yani avoided him. It was almost sweet if Yani was being perfectly honest with himself. He didn't want to be. He wanted the rock of anxiety and fear in his stomach to stay firmly lodged where it would keep him wary of Aaron and therefore keep himself safe.

Yani walked slowly toward Aaron, weaving through the tables of other patrons. He approached the table from the side as he dodged a group of frat boys desperately chugging down coffee to get rid of hangovers or whatever else ailed them.

Aaron's eyes were closed. He looked tired too. There were dark circles under his eyes, and his lips looked pinched as if it were taking effort to stay awake. Aaron looked so…the only way to put it was…human. Yani let out an inadvertent sigh. Aaron wasn't to blame for his father's mania, nor had he had a hand in Yani's kidnapping. He had even tried to stop the execution attempt despite not being sure Yani wasn't a vampire. The hard rock in Yani's stomach cracked and crumbled away. Yani could give Aaron a chance at the very least. If they couldn't get past this enough to date, then they could at least be friends.

The scrape of the second chair being pulled out from under the table jerked Aaron's eyes open. He looked up wildly, only relaxing when he saw Yani there.

"I didn't think you were going to come," he said softly as Yani sat.

"It wasn't your fault," Yani replied with a shrug. Aaron's shoulders relaxed slightly at Yani's words, moving down from his ears to a more comfortable position. "I shouldn't blame you for what your father did. I just needed time to process and forget."

Aaron grimaced. "I wouldn't have been surprised if you never wanted to see me again. You have no idea how sorry I am that I caused that."

"You told them over and over again that you met me in sunlight," Yani interjected. "You fought with them to get me free, and you finally succeeded. I don't think you really have anything to be sorry for. It's your father and the other radical people he works with who need to apologize." Yani was just repeating the argument he had been having with himself over Aaron for the last few hours. It was odd having to justify Aaron's actions to Aaron, but it was also comforting in a way to know that Aaron was just as upset about how that night had ended as Yani.

Aaron snorted. "They don't have the emotional capacity to realize they've done something wrong, let alone apologize to a human who accidentally got mixed up with their crap. I've always preferred the few months I got to stay with my mom," he added in an apparent non sequitur. "I mean, living with her was never fun because every conversation with her was about how awful my dad was. When I was a kid, I always thought she was just bitter and vindictive, but I know better now. I couldn't live with her all the way in Worcester and still keep up with college, but I scraped together all my savings and put a down payment on an apartment. I've moved out of the compound, and I've managed to convince my mother that this is a blow to my dad—which it kind of is—so she's paid my rent for the next three months while I'm working on finding a new job."

"Wow," Yani said because Aaron appeared to want him to say something. "You turned your back on your father because of what he did to me?"

Aaron didn't look happy, but he nodded. "I'm trying to distance myself as much as I can from what my dad stands for."

It was admirable, and Yani respected that. Yani felt they were back to square one, just sitting down for their first date and learning about each other. Yani really liked Aaron, and his body was telling Yani it wasn't just as friends.

"Well, what do we have here?" a sly voice interjected from over Yani's shoulder. Yani froze in place because he could never, ever forget that voice. It was low and overtly sexual, a bedroom voice at its most sultry, and it belonged to Luke. "Is my little snack out on a date?"

"Luke," Yani groaned, "please go away."

Aaron was staring behind Yani at Luke, and Yani couldn't blame him. Luke was so damned hot. His model-high cheekbones and rounded jaw, thick lips, and bright-blue eyes were perfection on a human face. He could mesmerize any gay boy in just a few seconds.

One long-fingered hand with black-painted nails reached for Yani's chin, gripping and gently turning his head so Yani could see Luke. All of Yani's protests faded away as those wide eyes focused on Yani's. Luke wanted to have sex, and Yani was amenable to that. Yani could feel himself getting hard, as he always did around Luke, his body pushing uncomfortably against the zipper in his jeans. He tilted his head back almost involuntarily, asking for a kiss that he knew from memory would taste sweet and make his knees melt.

Luke grinned, his sharp white teeth flashing between red lips, before bending forward to take what Yani was freely offering.

A hand appeared suddenly, cutting between their faces and clapping down forcefully over Yani's eyes. He blinked for a few seconds, trying to figure out what had happened to Luke and why they weren't kissing before he realized that those blue eyes were gone, and instead he was staring at the palm and fingers of someone's hand.

"I know you weren't ensnaring my nephew in your spell of lust, incubus," a voice Yani didn't recognize hissed threateningly. It was lightly accented, but the English was clear. "I wouldn't take kindly to knowing you were supping from him."

"Your nephew?" Luke replied, although the sultry tone Yani was used to hearing was gone. "I had no idea he was related to a master, honest!"

Magnified

The hand pulled away from Yani's eyes, moving to gently rest on his shoulder instead. Yani shook his head as if he had to clear his brain. When he looked up again, Luke was still standing in front of Yani, but he looked ordinary. None of the automatic lust and attraction Yani felt whenever Luke was near appeared. Luke was still very handsome, but in a normal "he should be a model or an actor" way. He was also staring, almost horrified, with wide, fearful eyes, behind Yani.

Yani craned his neck to look around and found his mirror double standing just behind him. Another man, the one Luke was staring at, was just removing his hand from covering Aaron's eyes.

"Uncle Yakov, Uncle Martin?" Yani asked tentatively.

Aaron blinked and shook his head before turning to look at Martin. "Vampire," he hissed, tensing in his seat although he couldn't jump up like Yani thought he wanted to thanks to Martin's hand on his shoulder.

"Mage," Martin replied with a polite nod of his head. "I would have thought you had learned the ability to protect against incubus attacks at your age," he added.

Aaron swallowed hard, but his jaw was firm. "Please remove your hand from my shoulder."

Martin complied, stepping away from Aaron until he stood next to Uncle Yakov. Aaron followed Martin with his eyes, but he didn't move until he caught sight of Yakov standing next to Yani.

"The photo," Aaron gasped, staring at Yakov. Shock overtook fear on his face.

"This is my uncle Yakov and his partner, Martin," Yani said politely to Aaron and Luke, who appeared to be frozen on the spot.

"Shit," Luke gasped, and winced a second later. "Look, I'm sorry. I didn't know!"

"You didn't know you were forcing sexual attentions on my nephew?" Martin asked sharply. "Even if Yani had not been my family, you should not be ensnaring any humans so callously."

Luke scoffed. "I'm an incubus. That's what we do."

Martin shook his head. "Find a willing partner who understands that you will be eating his sexual energy. I am certain you will find the right someone for you someday. It might not be when you expect it, but it will happen." He was staring at Yakov as he spoke the last sentence, and a small smile flitted across his lips. Yakov smiled back, widely and without restraint.

A soft beeping noise interrupted their moment, and Aaron dug his phone out of his pocket sheepishly. "Sorry. I've got a missed call and a voice mail message. Do you mind if I listen to it quickly? It's from the compound, but it's not my dad's number."

He sounded worried and his brows furrowed. Martin nodded, apparently catching the same cues Yani was seeing, and Aaron quickly hit a few buttons on the touch screen. The speakerphone wasn't on, but the volume was still loud enough that Yani could hear frantic breathing on the other end.

"Aaron, there's been an emergency," a woman's voice gasped. Her words were stilted, as if she was running and out of breath. "The vampires came back to life, but the door was open. We're overrun, and we need all fighters to come home immediately."

The call cut off suddenly with a loud crackle. A few seconds later, the phone beeped to indicate the message had ended.

"They closed the roof of the execution room when it rained a few days ago," Aaron breathed, shock making his voice breathy and worried.

Magnified

"Blood of the fallen and dark of the day brings back the dead whatever the fray," Martin replied cryptically. When Aaron looked blank-faced at him, Martin wordlessly reached down to pick up Yani's arm—the one that had bled into the vampire dust. "Shall we go investigate?"

"I'm not a hunter," Aaron said forcefully, even as he pushed his chair back and found his feet. "I don't kill vampires like the rest of them do."

"But your family is there," Yakov insisted.

Aaron led the way out of the café, weaving through tables and other patrons as quickly as he could. "They're not really a good family to have," Aaron tried to explain.

"Either way, someone must go quell the ravening vampires before they escape into the city proper," Martin interrupted as they stepped outside. "I should be able to do that with minimal bloodshed."

"What can I do to help?" Luke asked. He had followed them outside, although Yani hadn't noticed until now.

"Go to the local vampire coven," Martin replied. "Explain to the master what is occurring and ask him to please call on me before the night is over. I will be at the hunters' compound until dawn."

Luke swallowed hard in fear, but he gamely nodded. "I'll do that." He turned and jogged off down the street.

"We should probably hurry," Yakov insisted. He wrapped one arm around Yani's waist as he spoke.

"Yes, love," Martin agreed. "Pardon my forwardness," he added as he circled Aaron's waist with one arm too.

Yani felt Yakov crouch slightly, and then with a jolt that left Yani's stomach behind, they were airborne. They weren't flying, precisely, Yani realized as cars and buildings whipped by underneath them. Yakov was jumping, and the sheer strength in his legs was enough to glide them a fair distance before they dropped. Yakov had to push off a building to regain height and speed. It was much faster than traveling by car, particularly considering the constant Boston traffic. There must have been some sort of magic at play, because no one looked up or pointed as they flew by overhead. Soon they were out of the city proper, bouncing through suburbs and then empty fields. The long driveway and the lights of the compound came into view after another few minutes, and they landed smoothly on the doorstep.

Yakov let Yani go next to Aaron and stepped forward to stand next to Martin. "Do we just go in?" Yakov asked.

"Yes. We must watch out for hunters as well as ravening vampires. Be careful, love," Martin replied.

Martin pushed the front door open. It resisted for half a second before swinging open with a cracking sound. The deadbolt hung free in the wall from where it had been holding the door closed. Martin stepped over the threshold, Yakov only a step behind. Aaron slid in after them and Yani followed.

The entrance hall was completely empty and silent. It looked untouched, as if all the occupants of the house were safely elsewhere. A massive staircase filled the center of the room, connecting the upper floors to the front door. The floor was built of ornate marble that their shoes clacked against. The noise echoed through the room, emphasizing the lack of other sound.

"This way," Aaron insisted, quickly leading them to a small door tucked underneath the stairs. It looked like an old servant's door, and when Aaron pulled it open, a long, empty hallway that lacked all of the opulence of the entry hall behind them appeared. "The staircase and upstairs are a façade, just in case we're attacked. The main compound is through here."

Aaron led them down the hall at a jog, slow for the vampires, but Yani was just barely keeping up. While Yani was in good shape, Aaron was definitely in better condition. The hallway ended at a heavy steel door, propped open by a pair of unmoving legs. The feet were clad only in socks, and the hem of plaid pajama pants covered the ankles. Yani couldn't see the rest of the body until Martin pulled the door open.

He didn't recognize the pale, bloodless corpse that rolled free. There was a pair of puncture wounds underneath his chin and a gun lying at his side. The weapon hadn't saved him.

"We must hurry," Martin insisted. He said something else in a language Yani didn't recognize. Yakov responded immediately in the same language, and they both rushed forward. Had Yani blinked, he would have missed their departure entirely, they moved so quickly.

Aaron's face was completely blank as he stepped over the fallen man's body, but Yani had a feeling that Aaron was just covering up his true feelings. Aaron picked up the gun and followed the vampires farther into the compound.

Yani recognized the white walls of the hallway, including the unisex sign on the bathroom door as they hurried onward. They saw more dead bodies as they passed the destroyed door to the execution room. It was buckled in places, the hinges bent and broken, and leaning crookedly against the wall. The heavy spotlights inside the room showed a closed ceiling and an otherwise empty space. The pile of dust was gone, and someone had ripped the chains apart, leaving links of silver metal strewn about violently.

They could hear screaming now, and the pop of gunfire. Aaron picked up his pace, running toward the increasing noise. The hallway turned abruptly to the left, and the stark white of the walls ended just as suddenly. Bright carpet and walls filled what looked like a common living room. A gigantic TV laid smashed on the floor, and couches and tables were overturned. The carpet squished beneath his feet as Yani skidded to a stop behind Aaron.

Martin and Yakov were off to the left. Martin was moving quickly, approaching each ravening vampire and gripping it by the chin. He stared into the eyes of the vampire before releasing it. Whatever the vampire had been doing previously, drinking or killing, the vampire stopped and stepped away. Yakov was protecting Martin's back, and as Yani watched, he caught a crossbow bolt shot at Martin's head by the same man Yani recognized from his own short stay. The man was bleeding heavily from one arm and leaning against the wall for support, but he was alive, which couldn't be said for many others.

Aaron put his back to the nearest wall and started shooting at the vampires Martin hadn't already gotten to. One female vampire was laughing, her voice high and crazed, as she shook the two helpless adult hunters she was holding in the air by the front of their shirts. Aaron took out both of her shoulders, the double pop of his gun firing twice. Her scream as bone shattered and she dropped her intended victims to the floor echoed in Yani's ears.

Yakov caught a second crossbow bolt.

Yani grimly edged around Aaron and headed toward the man with the crossbow. Yani didn't know how to fire a gun—heck, this was the very first time he had ever seen one that wasn't in a museum. Picking up one of the dozen discarded ones on the floor wouldn't help. Stopping the idiot trying to kill Uncle Martin might actually do some good, and Yani couldn't simply stand in the doorway while everyone else was helping.

"Stop," he yelled over the screams, crying, and gunfire. He was trying to catch the man's attention, but the man was furiously trying to force his injured arm to steady his crossbow while he loaded another arrow. "They're friends. They're trying to help!"

"They're vampires," the man snarled, spittle flying from his mouth to join the pool of blood quickly growing below him. "They must be killed."

Yani reached the man and knocked the crossbow to the ground. "You can't kill someone just because he's a vampire," Yani insisted when the man snarled and glared. He clearly didn't have the energy to bend and retrieve his crossbow, so he settled for glaring heavily at Yani instead.

"You brought this upon us," the man continued crazily. "Your evil ties to the vampire destroyed us all!"

He probably meant how much Yani looked like Uncle Yakov, but if what Martin had alluded to, that his blood in the vampire dust had given the vampires the strength to revive, then the man wasn't too far off. Still, Yani hadn't had any part in creating that pile of dust to begin with.

"You brought this on yourself," Yani snarled back, unable to keep his temper in check. "You indiscriminately killed vampires for no reason other than hate. How would you behave if you suddenly came back to life after being tortured to death?"

The man snarled again but didn't answer. His eyes were flickering shut and his face was very pale. Blood loss was taking its toll.

"Yani, watch out!" Aaron's voice yelled frantically. Yani half turned in Aaron's direction and saw him lift his gun to point at something behind Yani. Yani spun around. A vampire was descending from the ceiling, falling directly at Yani in what seemed like slow motion. In fact, everything slowed, the constant screams muffled and distorted, as the vampire drew closer inch by inch.

His fangs were bared and bloody, his eyes crazed and vacant but fixed on Yani. A gun fired. The bullet whizzed by, missing by a hair's breadth just as one clawed hand touched Yani's cheek.

Sound and motion returned to Yani with a jolt and the vampire returned to normal speed, his mouth opening wider as he aimed for Yani's neck. And then, suddenly, he was gone.

Yani gasped and belatedly tried to duck. He glanced up when pain didn't strike to see Luke and Brandon wrestling the vampire away. The room was filled with a dozen more people, all of whom were throwing the vampires away from the humans and holding them steady for Martin to approach.

A man wearing plastic gloves and carrying what looked like a medical kit hurried past Yani toward where crossbow man was still slumped against the wall. Other medics were approaching the wounded as Martin continued to hurry to each vampire in turn.

"Are you okay?" Aaron gasped. He was panting for breath, almost wheezing, as he stopped at Yani's side.

Yani shook his head. Physically he was unharmed, but mentally? Oh, there would be nightmares. Yani knew that already.

"I'll be all right," Yani finally answered. "What about you?" Aaron didn't answer, but his face was still horribly blank.

"Why are you bandaging that vampire?" a woman's shrill voice yelled over the quickly diminishing sounds of screams and sobs. "I've got a broken arm and leg, and you're keeping a vampire from bleeding out? Ridiculous!"

The doctor in question was helping the vampire with the wounded shoulders that Aaron had shot. The doctor turned his head to glare at the shrill-sounding hunter and hissed, a pair of retractable fangs and a forked tongue becoming very evident as his mouth opened. The woman fell silent immediately with a gasp.

Martin finished with the last vampire, and he and Yakov walked over to Yani and Aaron. An older gentleman and a young woman joined them a moment later. She waved Brandon over. Luke hurried over too.

"Yani?" Brandon gasped when he reached them. "What are you doing here?"

Yani frowned at Brandon. "I thought you had a family dinner tonight," he said pointedly.

The older man cleared his throat deliberately and raised one white eyebrow at Brandon.

"Grandfather," Brandon said immediately. "I believe I've told you about my college roommate, Yani."

Yakov started laughing, one hand politely covering his mouth as he leaned on Martin. "Oh, nephew. You do make things interesting. Your roommate is a werewolf, your ex-lover an incubus, and you're dating a mage. However did you manage that?"

Yani just shook his head, overwhelmed and, quite frankly, clueless. He had no idea that he had a deep connection to the supernatural world. Aside from vampires, he hadn't even known more magical creatures existed.

"You are Sir Martin Wielki, of Bedzin, Poland?" the older man asked very politely.

Martin nodded his head, the sort of regal nod Yani only ever saw in movies about medieval kings or fantasy realms. "I was once called that, yes, but it has been nearly a thousand years since that time. Please, call me Martin. This is my partner, Yakov, and his nephew Yani Goldhaber. I would appreciate if you could explain what has been happening here in Boston that Yani felt the need to contact us."

"I am Bishop Karr, alpha of the Charles River Pack and the current President of the Supernatural Coalition of the Northeast. These are two of my grandchildren, Janet and Brandon Karr. About fifteen years ago, this hunter compound cropped up. We observed them at first but found them to be ineffective and easily avoided. They were more of a nuisance than an actual concern. Three years ago, that changed. The master vampire of the local coven vanished, and one by one the coven itself began to disappear as well. Our investigation recently proved the hunter compound to be at the center of the trouble, and we were in the process of devising a method of apprehending them with minimal casualties on both sides. You beat us to the game, as you can see, but I honestly can't complain about that." He paused to take a deep breath and then shook his head. "We will begin a trial at once to ensure the culprits are properly punished and the coven receives retribution."

At that moment the same woman from before began screaming again. "What do you think you're doing? Let me go!" Her good arm was being handcuffed to another mostly uninjured hunter.

"Ma'am, you are under arrest for the illegal incarceration and execution of two and a half dozen innocent vampires," the woman locking the handcuffs insisted. "You will receive a fair trial."

Gurneys were brought down to roll the injured away. Those hunters still mobile were led away in cuffs while the vampires were gently led to another room.

"There should be children hidden in safe rooms inside almost every apartment," Aaron called to a group of guards who didn't look busy, while pointing toward a doorway where the majority of the hunters had congregated during the fight. "The override code is four zero eight two star."

"Traitor," a man in cuffs snarled, but Aaron ignored him. Aaron's face still held that horrible blankness as he continued to survey the room.

All of a sudden, that mask cracked. Tears pooled in Aaron's eyes as his lower lip began to tremble. "Dad?" he asked the air. Yani turned toward where Aaron was looking to see a heavy couch being lifted off Aaron's father's prone body. Aaron took off across the room at a sprint, dodging prisoners and patients alike as he hurried to his father's side. Yani followed, his legs moving almost involuntarily.

There was blood everywhere, Yani saw with horrible realization as he drew close to Aaron's dad. The couch was completely out of the way, and one of the helpers tried to stop Aaron as he dropped to his knees at his father's side.

"Dad?" Aaron repeated breathlessly, his voice choked and his hand shaking as he reached out slowly.

Yani stepped next to Aaron and had to swallow hard to stop himself from gagging and throwing up. Aaron's dad hadn't been sucked dry like the first corpse in the doorway. He hadn't been beaten or broken like many of the hunters currently surrounding them. No, someone had simply torn his throat out and left him to die. No fanfare, no ravening hunger. Just dead and forgotten, much as the hunter had so callously done to so many vampires.

Yani stumbled away, falling to his knees in an empty corner where he promptly and violently emptied his stomach all over the blood-spotted carpet and wall.

"Come away," Yakov said gently, one hand carefully pulling Yani to his feet and then across the room. All that was left was blood and destruction. Even the dead bodies were being carted away. Brandon and Luke were trying to get Aaron to his feet too, Yani saw, but weren't having much success until a doctor rushed over with a syringe, and Aaron collapsed as the sedation took quick effect.

"The vampires will remain under my control until the sun rises," Martin was explaining to Bishop. "I have willed them to tell the truth as they saw it of their last nights alive, so be certain to get their statements quickly."

"Of course," Bishop replied in thanks. "How long do you think you will be staying in Boston? The supernatural community could use a master vampire of your strength living here."

"For as long as my dear Yakov can stand it, which will most likely be only so long as Yani needs our aid," Martin replied with a smile. "Now, if you will excuse me, I believe we both have important things to take care of before the night is over."

Martin hurried to Luke and Brandon, who had been levering Aaron's body onto a gurney the doctor had hastily brought over. "I shall take charge of this one," he insisted, pushing away the handcuffs one guard was opening to put around Aaron's slack wrists. He gathered Aaron in his arms, nodded to Yakov, who also picked Yani up, and they both left the bloodstained room behind.

Yani let his eyes slide shut, trying to block the remembered images of death and blood that appeared there. He didn't know when he passed out, but darkness took him away quickly.

Martin walked into the upstairs bedroom and to Yakov's side. He put one comforting hand on Yakov's shoulder and waited in silence. There were two twin-sized beds in the room, and tucked under the covers were Yani and Aaron. Both were passed out, one from human drugs and the other from shock.

"I was never that innocent," Yakov said sadly, gazing down at Yani, who looked so very much like him, especially with his face looking so ashen. "I never had so much innocence to lose in one fell swoop."

"A sign of the times, I believe, as well as the fact that thanks to the existence of Israel a second Holocaust against the Jews is impossible." Martin drew Yakov backward into his arms where he could hold him tightly. "And yet, Yani comes from a line of survivors. You survived, beloved, Chana survived, and together all of your children survived and eventually thrived. I do not believe Yani will do anything less. Now, darling, let us allow them to rest."

Martin guided Yakov out of the bedroom and down two flights of stairs until they reached the basement. At first glance, the basement appeared ordinary, but a well-concealed trapdoor in the floor led to a comfortable daytime resting place. Martin had had the foresight to purchase the house years ago, in case Yakov's family ever needed him, and had it outfitted for their use.

"How did the meeting with the rest of the Supernatural Coalition go?" Yakov asked once the trapdoor was secured again. The sun would be rising within the hour.

Martin shook his head sadly. "At least a third of the coven is still missing despite the hunters' compound being searched quite thoroughly. There is also the mystery of the sudden increase in the hunters' abilities, which is under investigation as well. We've yet to discover the larger picture here, my love, but we shall figure it all out in due time."

Yakov sighed. "I hope so. What did they say in regards to Yani and Aaron?"

"They are part of the supernatural world now—there is no escaping that—but the coalition is willing to allow both children to simply live. Should they join their friends Luke and Brandon or not, I have been given assurances that it will be entirely their choice."

"That is good to know," Yakov said, sounding relieved. "You should rest. You expended a lot of energy tonight, and I know it's been a few days since you've fed."

Martin smiled fondly at Yakov, drawing him close with one hand before bending down to firmly kiss him. "I am sure you are hungry too. When the sun sets, we shall go hunting."

"That does sound nice," Yakov agreed.

They kissed again, Martin gently holding Yakov in his arms in order to enjoy the familiar feel of those warm lips against his own, but the oncoming sun broke them apart far too soon for Martin's tastes. He led Yakov over to their shared bed and held the covers back so Yakov could get settled before climbing in after him and pulling him close. The sun touched the horizon, and involuntary sleep took them both away.

Three: Peace

The polke had barely started to digest in Yani's stomach before Christmas music began blaring from every set of speakers in Boston. Admittedly, the giant turkey drumstick he had eaten along with generous helpings of stuffing, green beans, sweet potatoes, mashed potatoes, cranberry sauce, and lots of desserts hadn't helped with the digestion process, but there was no reason for the music to start playing so soon. He stepped off the bus in Boston after spending a nice Thanksgiving at home, and the bus station was playing it over the loudspeaker. Yani had no idea why it had to be played so incessantly throughout the whole of December. He was already tired of it, and December had barely begun.

Even the café had succumbed.

"They're obviously late. Do you want to sneak into the bathroom and have a quickie while we're waiting?"

Yani turned his head from where he had been watching the sidewalk out the window to glare at Luke. Luke hadn't used any of his powers on Yani since Uncle Martin had scolded him, but that didn't stop him from asking about sex every time they met, which was fairly often these days. Although sometimes it seemed as if Luke was only asking because he knew Yani would always say no.

"You have a boyfriend," Yani sighed. "And I've got… whatever the heck it is with Aaron."

Luke snorted. "'Whatever the heck it is' is right! I know you haven't had sex with him, and I'm pretty sure you haven't even given each other so much as a hand job. It's sad."

"And you and Brandon are already having sex?" Yani asked, although it was pretty easy to assume. Luke just smiled lasciviously, the seductive tilt to his lips more than enough answer for Yani.

From what Yani had later been told, it was love at first sight for Luke and Brandon. Luke stumbled into the Supernatural Coalition's headquarters, yelling about vampires going rogue at the hunter compound and a master vampire who was hurrying to stop them. Bishop, Brandon's grandfather, took control of the situation and handed Luke off to Brandon to care for while he mustered the troops. Supposedly, their eyes met in the confusion and they just knew they were right for each other. It had something to do with mating; a werewolf always knew who their mate was, and an incubus could read lust and love emotions like no other creature. At least, that was the little Yani had been able to learn. He was too new to the supernatural world to really understand all of it, but he was trying.

Finally, the bell over the door sounded, clashing jarringly with the notes in the Christmas carol currently playing on the loudspeakers. Brandon and Aaron stopped by the counter first, grabbing coffee to warm their chilled fingers. Aaron put his cup down in front of the chair next to Yani and began the lengthy process of pulling off gloves, scarf, hat, and coat.

"It's really cold out there," Aaron gasped, rubbing his hands together briskly to force some warmth back into them. Once his heavy winter wear was tucked onto the back of his chair, he sat and picked up his warm cup of coffee again. Even though the temperatures were still mostly above freezing during the day this time of year, the constant wind off the harbor ensured fingers and toes were always frozen.

"Hello to you too," Yani griped jokingly. Aaron and Yani weren't dating—they weren't really anything but good friends at the moment—but there was something more brewing between them. Every time their eyes caught, Yani's heart beat a little faster and his breath stuttered in his chest.

It started at Aaron's dad's funeral when only Aaron and his mother attended from among his dad's friends and family. The supernatural community sent a representative and Mary came with Yani, Luke, and Brandon to support Aaron, but it really sent home the fact that Aaron's dad had been alone and bitter. Had Aaron stayed with him for much longer, he might have suffered the same fate.

Aaron reached out and took Yani's hand in his during the service, clutching it tightly until Yani started to lose feeling in his fingers. Aaron needed the comfort and somehow knew that despite their unfortunate history Yani would give it. Yani had Aaron's hand in his and thought about the fragile warmth of it, what it really meant, and how his heart automatically beat faster at the contact. Some of Yani's thoughts weren't appropriate for a funeral, but they made one thing very clear: Yani was interested in Aaron.

Aaron's answering grin was wide and playful. It was also a huge step up from what Yani saw even a few days ago. Aaron had taken his father's death hard, and it took a while for him to smile at anyone. Yani knew that having a new purpose for his life—finding the person who had set his father on the dark path that eventually killed him—allowed Aaron to begin to move past his pain. Aaron wasn't healed yet and wouldn't be for a very long while, but every day got a little better for him, and he fought not to let any of that depression into his life. Yani had no doubt it was a constant struggle, but Aaron was strong and wouldn't let it bog him down.

"Hello. I figured you wouldn't mind being distracted from that," Aaron said with a pointed tilt of his head toward their table companions. Brandon hadn't taken off any of his winter clothing yet; instead, he had set his coffee on the table and his butt in Luke's lap. They were currently trying to eat each other's tonsils.

Brandon wasn't a big guy, but he had the build of someone who was very active. He had a thin frame that helped to hide his muscles, but Yani knew he was very strong. They had been living together in the dorms for two years now, so Yani knew all about Brandon's six-pack. His hair was colored dirty blond and Brandon never did anything with it, leaving him looking scruffy, which was all the better for Luke to bury his hands there while they were kissing. Brandon hadn't come out as gay to Yani—in fact, he'd never had a girlfriend or boyfriend that Yani could think of, but it was all too obvious what Brandon's sexual preference was now.

Yani rolled his eyes at the display and turned toward Aaron instead. He looked older when Yani saw his eyes and the weight on his shoulders, but he also had a purpose in life. Someone had guided his father's overzealous hand, and Aaron wanted to find out whom in order to avenge his father's death. Since that was in line with the Supernatural Coalition's plans, Yani knew that was why he was working for them and, quite honestly, was enjoying the position.

Another Christmas song started playing over the speakers, and Yani couldn't help sighing and groaning to himself. Aaron pulled his cup away from his mouth and grinned again.

"It's 'Silent Night.' Come on, you can't hate 'Silent Night.'"

Yani grimaced again before replying. "It's beautiful, don't get me wrong, but do you know how many times I've heard it just today? Everyone who thinks they have talent in the music business puts out 'Silent Night' as a holiday single. I've heard four different versions of the same facacta song just today. Where's the originality?"

"Weren't most Christmas songs written by Jews?" Aaron asked slowly, as if he wasn't sure he should continue the conversation. Given that Yani was swearing in Yiddish, his concern wasn't too off base.

Yani couldn't help laughing at himself, his heavy mood slipping away. "A large majority of them, yes. 'Rudolf' is Jewish, but 'Silent Night' isn't." It was a source of quiet pride for the American Jewish community that so much of their art was considered mainstream—not in terms of assimilation, but rather the fact that religion wasn't a factor when it came to appreciation of their skills. It was a trait that was fairly unique to the US, but greatly prized all the same.

Brandon and Luke eventually separated. They didn't find their own chairs, but Brandon did get his coat and mittens off so he could enjoy his coffee.

"So, why did you call us here?" Aaron asked once he and Brandon started to look rosy-cheeked instead of pale and slightly frostbitten.

Brandon was using Luke's chest as a backrest, but that didn't diminish from the sudden intenseness that filled his eyes and straightened his spine. "Grandpa's found something, and he wants us to come in tonight to see if we can make heads or tails of it."

He pulled out his smartphone and hit a few buttons before turning it to show them a picture. Aaron leaned forward, his eyes intent as he read the words written there.

It looked like a photo of a yellowed and slightly cracked page from a really old book. There had been a picture drawn at the top of the page, but the ink was faded and smudged. All Yani could make out was a vaguely human shape. Below that were the words Aaron was so intent on. They looked like an odd mixture between Hebrew, Arabic, and hieroglyphics.

Before all of the supernatural stuff had entered Yani's life, seeing Hebrew so blatantly used for spells and such would have been massively offensive to him. All too often in fantasy literature, Hebrew and the Jewish Star were used in evil spells to summon the devil or to hurt people. Whether it was ignorance or anti-Semitism on the part of the author and artist was irrelevant because either way it was wrong and hurtful. Yet Yani found now that the older the language and culture, the more likely it was to be entwined with some sort of ancient mysticism.

Hebrew wasn't used to exclusively summon the devil, no, but if a mage happened to live in the Middle East two thousand plus years ago, then his grimoires, good or bad, were most likely written in ancient Hebrew. Or, like the spell Yani couldn't make heads or tails of, were written in whatever languages were indigenous to the area at the time.

"This isn't the full spell," Aaron said. He was still studying the photo as he spoke.

Brandon shook his head. "Grandpa said I could only take a picture of one page and that I have to delete it when I'm done."

"Smart," Aaron replied. "This is the middle section of a binding spell to forcibly tie a supernatural creature from another plane to this world and to the bidding of the summoner. It could be a stereotypical demon summoning, but there are plenty of other, equally dangerous creatures out there. Without the full spell, I can't tell you what you're looking at."

"Where did you learn all that?" Yani couldn't help asking, impressed with Aaron's knowledge.

Aaron grinned slightly, looking up at Yani with mischief in his eyes. He mumbled something under his breath, and the spoon in Yani's coffee stirred twice in a circle without anyone touching it. Yani gaped at him, shocked. Why hadn't he known Aaron had magical powers? Although now that he was thinking about it, he should have. Uncle Martin had called Aaron a mage often enough, and it wasn't his history as a hunter that had caused the coalition to recruit him.

"My mom's a witch. My dad had powers, too, which was how he could make those spelled manacles, but he was never as strong as Mom and me. That's how they met, at a witches' convention."

"I thought your mom was Jewish?" Brandon asked curiously.

Aaron's grin widened. "You ever hear of something called Kabbalah? Not the Hollywood version, but real Jewish mysticism? Back in ancient times, people like my mother would have been part of it. Today she's just a witch, and old, super-religious men with no powers study the ancient texts instead."

Yani had been to Tz'fat, the capital of Kabbalah in Israel, during a family trip there a few years ago and knew exactly what Aaron was referring to. He had never considered the idea that thousands of years ago the people who had practiced Kabbalah actually had powers, but it was certainly interesting to learn now.

Aaron's grin faded as he glanced back at the photo. "This isn't anything so benign, though. It calls for the violent and painful death of at least three people. Very dark and very malevolent. Whoever used this spell is not good news."

Hearing Aaron talk about killing people for power while the speakers overhead were gently singing out the last lines of "Silent Night" presented a painful dichotomy. Torturing and killing people for a binding spell. "Sleep in heavenly peace, sleep in heavenly peace."

Yani believed Aaron, of course, and the spell seemed to radiate an evil sort of aura even from Brandon's phone, but he couldn't help feeling left out of the conversation. He was the only one at the table without any background in magic. Brandon and Luke both seemed to understand most of what Aaron was explaining while Yani was only getting the basic gist. For the first time, Yani felt like he didn't belong.

The bell over the café door chimed again. Yani looked up, desperate for some sort of distraction, and saw Mary and Ettie walking inside. The girls spotted their group almost immediately. Mary waved with a smile, but headed to the counter to get something warm first. Since Brandon wasn't actually using the fourth chair at the table, they only needed to find one more seat. Yani scooted his chair closer to Aaron to make room for Mary to sit. Ettie took the empty side of the table. Mary had a small hot chocolate warming her hands. Ettie had a large cocoa and a couple of sugarcoated Danishes.

"Troll," Luke said.

"Incubus," Ettie replied with a nod of her head. Yani had always thought those were insults about their looks hurled cruelly every time the two met, but now he knew better. They were just statements of fact though Yani didn't know why Luke and Ettie persisted in calling each other by their species instead of their names.

"So we're interrupting a boys' day out?" Mary asked. She was eyeing how close Yani's chair was to Aaron's, and Yani had little doubt she thought she was interrupting a double date. That hadn't stopped her from coming over anyway, of course. Her wide grin confirmed that she wanted all the gossip.

Brandon's phone had vanished when the girls came over. He seemed relieved to have the discussion finished for the moment. "I don't know... Are they interrupting anything?" he asked Luke slyly, shifting his weight on Luke's lap with a seductive glance up at Luke's face through his eyelashes.

Aaron hid a smile in his coffee. Yani, after long experience being around Luke, already knew what was going to come out of Luke's mouth. He gave a preemptive groan and buried his face in one hand.

"My mama always told me," Luke said, his voice perfectly ordinary, but when Yani peeked between his fingers, he could see the sparkle in Luke's eyes, "that she wouldn't bail me out of jail for getting caught having sex in public. My dick could be buried in sweet Brandon's ass right now, but I wouldn't be able to tell you thanks to Mama's orders." He rolled his hips forward, as if he really were thrusting deep, all while grinning at Mary.

"And that was crude and unnecessary," Mary grumbled over Aaron and Brandon's laughter.

"Then let's not hang around them any longer," Ettie rumbled with a heavy frown leveled at Luke. She apparently didn't approve of incubi. Yani wondered if there was some sort of animosity between the two species. Her cocoa and sweets were already long gone. Mary gulped the last of her own cocoa and stood.

"Tony's probably already waiting for us anyway. See you at dinner?"

Yani looked at Brandon for confirmation. He didn't know when they were supposed to head over to the Supernatural Headquarters. Brandon nodded.

"Sure," Yani agreed, happy that he was getting the chance to spend more time with his friends. Mary left with another pointed look between Yani and Aaron. The conversation didn't pick up again once the girls left. There wasn't much more they could talk about without Aaron seeing the rest of the grimoire. They bundled up again for the cold and threw away their trash on the way out the door.

"It's still fall," Brandon groaned as they stepped outside and a gust of cold wind immediately battered against them. The weather was unseasonably cold for late autumn. Yes, the winter coats would be out of the back of the closet by this point, but the heavy hats, scarves, and mittens shouldn't be. This was January weather.

"I'll warm you up," Luke replied, his voice husky as his arms pulled Brandon closer. Their lips met, and Yani could see tongues tangling before he managed to look away. He and Brandon were heading back to the dorms together, so he had to wait for their lengthy, and loud, goodbye to end.

"Werewolves," Aaron sighed at Yani's side. "They can never keep it in their pants, I swear."

"Werewolves?" Yani asked. "I thought it was incubi who couldn't?"

Aaron laughed, one hand resting on Yani's shoulder for balance. "Oh, you are so right. A werewolf and an incubus mating is the perfect combination. The two randiest species." He kept laughing, unconsciously leaning more of his weight on Yani. Aaron's body was warm and his grip strong. His touch heated Yani's insides with want.

"I don't think I get the joke," Yani said, trying to distract himself.

Aaron's grinning face turned toward Yani, his eyes sparkling with mirth. Yani's heart thumped a little harder at the sight. "You should ask Brandon how many siblings he has. And how many aunts and uncles and cousins. Trust me, werewolves can't keep it in their pants, and Brandon mating with Luke is totally hilarious."

It was nice to hear his friends were happy, but Yani wanted to know whether Aaron wanted to try the human equivalent of mating with Yani. Or at the very least go on another date? It wasn't like before when they were both trying to keep Mary happy or to apologize for something. After weeks of just being friends, Yani knew what he wanted: a chance with Aaron. He ought to open his mouth and say it. Invite Aaron out for coffee, just the two of them without Luke and Brandon as a buffer. At the same time, Yani didn't want to ruin their current friendship. What if Aaron wasn't interested in Yani the same way?

Before Yani could make a decision, Brandon broke away from Luke and walked over to Yani's side. Luke turned and sauntered off with an extra twitch in his hips because he knew Brandon was watching his ass beneath his jacket.

"For your information, I am child number five of twelve. My parents are very disappointed they won't get any grandkids out of me, but since they already have seven, I think they'll survive." Brandon was grinning good-naturedly as he explained. "Now shoo, witch," he added with a flap of his hands in Aaron's direction. "Yani and I have homework to do."

Yani groaned at the reminder. He was only halfway through writing his essay, and the rough draft was due in a week. He could skip handing in a finished draft, but he wanted the input from his professor. His paper had turned too depressing for him to sit and write the entire thing in one swoop. Thousands of people had starved to death thanks to the extreme Communist policies in China and Ukraine, and even more had been killed when they tried to circumvent or fight against the system so they could survive. The most surprising part of his paper was just how stable the Communist governments themselves were. The leaders on top and their supporters were fine, which meant the government was working optimally, and that inevitably meant the West wasn't willing to intervene where they couldn't get a good foothold or exert their own influence. Yani could only work on the report for maybe an hour at a time before he had to take a mental health break.

"Have fun," Aaron said. He shot one last smile at Yani, which Yani immediately returned, before turning and walking in the direction of his apartment. Yani sighed, annoyed that he hadn't taken the chance to sound out Aaron on the dating idea, and followed Brandon back to the dorms.

The Supernatural Coalition was located north of Boston, where large plots of land weren't at a premium and forests weren't too hard to come by. The building was a large mansion tucked into an old forest. They had multiple floors underground, where the sunlight couldn't reach their nocturnal members, as well as a variety of other space for other creatures. Yani had heard there were two heated pools enclosed on the property: one for visiting freshwater creatures and the other for saltwater creatures.

The coalition itself was fairly isolated, but even far flung neighbors spied over the hedge occasionally. Which was one of the reasons Alpha Karr and the Charles River Pack owned the equally extensive property next door. Somewhere buried farther in the woods was a house owned by the Boston vampire coven. In fact, much of the small New England town was comprised of supernatural beings. They were safer in numbers, and it was wise to be physically involved with the politics that could define their way of life. A council without vampires might accidentally choose to do something important during the day, for example. That wasn't so different from the taxation without representation issue that had sparked the Revolutionary War, and since there were plenty of creatures in the coalition who had lived during that time period, they all made sure to be fully represented by staying close.

One of Brandon's uncles was coming home from work in Boston and was happy to stop and pick up Yani, Brandon, and Aaron on his way. Luke had his own means of travel and promised to meet them there. Once they escaped city traffic, the drive was quick and easy as it was only about twenty miles out of the city.

Brandon had taken the front seat, which left Yani sitting in the back next to Aaron. The ride was silent, but every once in a while Yani would turn his head and catch Aaron just looking away from him. Aaron wanted something from Yani, his hidden stare insisted, but what, specifically, was a mystery. Yani knew what he wanted it to be, but he was afraid the truth was the opposite. The drive ended before he could make up his mind to speak—not that he wanted to bring up their relationship issues in front of an audience anyway.

Brandon's uncle dropped them off at the coalition and then continued on home. The front door swung open as the car pulled away, and Luke hurried forward to yank Brandon into his arms.

"Hello, sexy," Luke growled as his hands slid slowly down Brandon's back to cup his ass and squeeze.

Aaron sighed and walked around them, heading into the building. Yani hurried to follow.

"Alpha Karr, I'm sure Brandon will only be a few minutes," Aaron was saying as Yani walked through the foyer and into a small sitting room off to the left. It was the general receiving room for the coalition, the only room of the house Yani had seen in all his visits. There was a merrily burning fireplace along one wall with two couches and three overstuffed armchairs placed around it. A small coffee table filled the middle of the room. Bishop Karr stood next to the mantle over the fire. He looked resigned at Aaron's explanation.

Lara Karr, Bishop's wife, giggled from where she was sitting in one of the armchairs. "Let them have their fun while they're still young," she insisted. "It's good you see you again, Aaron, Yani. I left a phone message with your uncles to see if they might be interested in seeing the book as well. I'm sure they'll arrive within the hour."

Lara sat with her back perfectly straight despite the puffy chair inviting her to relax. Her white hair was pulled into a tight bun at the nape of her neck, the tautness inadvertently displaying the heavy wrinkles around her mouth and eyes. They were from laugh lines, however, so she looked dignified and kind despite her otherwise stern appearance.

Yani pulled off his heavy winter clothes and draped them over the back of the chair by the door with Aaron's things before joining Aaron on the couch across from Lara. The couch wasn't big, so Yani had to sit close to Aaron's side. Their shoulders involuntarily brushed, and Yani had to hide a shiver of want.

Lara's smiled widened. "Are you two ever going to date?" she asked lightly. She would have looked innocent except for the slight tilt to her lips. She was a lot like Mary, wanting all the gossip. "I can smell how much you want each other," she added, her voice insistent as she gently tapped the tip of her nose with one finger.

Yani felt his cheeks going red as his face heated. A sideways glance at Aaron showed a similar reaction. Aaron shifted awkwardly in his seat before meeting Yani's eyes.

There was lust there, and it was definitely focused directly on Yani. There was no mistaking the want lingering there either—how had Yani missed it earlier?—nor the fact that Yani's eyes were conveying the same message in return. Aaron's eyes widened slightly as he looked at Yani, and one hand slowly reached out to gently touch Yani's knee. His head tilted slightly to the side, as if he were asking if Yani was okay with him being so close. Yani couldn't stop a smile from lifting his lips in response.

"Honestly, Lara. Can't you leave well enough alone?" Bishop interrupted, jarring Yani out of his mental connection with Aaron.

"There's nothing wrong with a little matchmaking," Lara insisted. "Especially when I can tell that all they needed was a little confirmation of their feelings. See?"

Bishop grumbled under his breath for a few seconds. Aaron's hand jumped away from Yani's knee in his surprise when Bishop first spoke, but it slowly returned to touch Yani's hand. Yani turned his palm over, inviting Aaron to clasp his hand.

They were still holding hands, and Lara was still beaming proudly for herself when Luke and Brandon finally walked into the parlor a few minutes later. Yakov and Martin were just behind them.

"Lovely, everyone's here," Lara exclaimed. She stood from her seat and walked to the door. "I'll let you get on to business. I've got that cute selkie to see to anyway."

She closed the parlor door behind her. Bishop nodded in greeting to Martin and Yakov before turning around. He did something that made a popping noise to the side of the fireplace, Yani couldn't see what, but all of a sudden an electronic keypad appeared in the brick. Bishop quickly input a code that caused the keypad to beep twice and a section of wall on the other side of the fireplace to slide open like a door.

"Follow me," Bishop instructed as he walked around the mantel toward the door. He pulled it farther open so everyone could fit through and then disappeared inside. Yani joined the group as everyone moved to follow. There was a long, steep staircase on the other side of the door. As Bishop walked down the stairs, lights in the walls flickered on. The bottom was still shrouded in darkness.

Brandon and Luke followed next. Aaron grinned at Yani and hurried after them. Since he was still holding Yani's hand, Yani was pulled along too.

"I see an interesting development has emerged," Yakov said quietly from a step or two behind Yani. Yani turned his head slightly so he could see Yakov without tripping on the stairs. Yakov was looking pointedly at where Aaron and Yani's hands were tightly gripped.

"It's, um…" Yani felt his cheeks get hot. "Very new," he finished quickly. "We haven't really talked about it yet."

"Be sure you do speak about it soon," Yakov instructed firmly, before falling silent again.

The door above them slid closed, encasing the stairs in only the scant light from the sconces in the wall. Bishop was still descending. Eventually, they reached a landing, which had one closed door in the wall. The stairs continued downward. Bishop didn't even pause at the door, instead turning the corner and continuing down the stairs.

Yani didn't want to know how deep underground they were by the time Bishop ran out of stairs. They had to be well below the coalition building, including the lightproof basement for nocturnal creatures. There was a heavy door at the foot of the stairs with another keypad glowing slightly in the dim light. Bishop tapped in a code and the door unlocked with a clunking sound.

Bishop covered his hand with a bit of cloth before he pushed the silver door open. He held it open while everyone walked into the dark room beyond. Yani could see just how thick the door was as he walked by; in fact, it looked like a vault door from a bank. On the back of the door was a heavy crossbar, currently open, but it was probably what had clunked when the lock disengaged. Once everyone was inside, Bishop let the door swing closed.

The room was completely dark, now that the lights from the hallway didn't illuminate anything. Yani couldn't help gripping Aaron's hand a little tighter in his as his eyes strained to see even the slightest bit. The clunking noise came again as the door locked, and then low lights in the floor turned on and began to brighten. The change in the darkness was gradual, but Yani was grateful for the slowness all the same. He might have been blinded had Bishop turned all the lights on at once.

Once the low lights in the floor reached full brightness, a second set in the ceiling began to glow. Yani's eyes quickly adjusted and he glanced around. The room was huge—massive to the point of feeling cavernous. Yani estimated that the far wall was at least a quarter mile away. Filling the space were hundreds of bookshelves, and each shelf was crammed full with books and scrolls. The closest shelf to Yani contained what looked like modern bound books, but for some reason a black aura seemed to emanate from the shelf. To Yani's left was a wooden banquet table. There were stacks of books filling the closest end. On the far side was a lone text sitting in front of the head of the table. Bishop led them there.

"Our librarian has been cataloguing the books we found in the hunters' compound," Bishop explained as he walked. "We moved the more volatile ones down here where they would be secure, of course." He pointed to the stacks of books at the end of the table. "This book, however, we located hidden in a secret compartment in the room belonging to the compound's leader. Of all the spells still legible, our experts believe we have narrowed our target down to just one. However, we lack the knowledge to decipher the spell fully."

"There was no one capable of translating the spell in the coalition?" Martin asked curiously, looking at the book sitting innocuously on the table. The book matched the picture Brandon had shown them earlier that day. The cover was brown, worn, and cracked. It looked old, but it also looked unremarkable.

Bishop grimaced and shook his head. "There is one woman who lives six hours away by car. However, she is the type of mage who would be interested in preforming such a dark spell. It wouldn't be wise to bring her here."

"Ah, no," Martin agreed dryly.

"Luckily, Aaron knows most of the ancient languages of magic," Bishop continued. He waved Aaron over, but everyone crowded close to see too. There were soft cloths on the table next to the book. Bishop used one cloth to carefully open the fragile book and turn to the correct page. Aaron let go of Yani's hand so he could bend over the book with his hands braced on the table for balance. It looked like he didn't want to even touch the book.

There was an oddly shaped stain on the first page Aaron was reading from. It could have been from ink, but Yani's imagination thought the stain was faintly reddish in color.

"This is an evil spell," Aaron murmured softly. His forehead was wrinkled in thought, and his mouth twisted in disgust as he read. "Blood of the innocent, blood of the damned. That's two people killed just to begin the spell. Their blood needs to be mixed and used to set the spell circle. There are more deaths later on." Aaron looked slightly green around the gills as he spoke.

"Don't bother reading too much into how the spell was performed," Bishop insisted. "Our librarian could read enough to know it's an evil spell, but couldn't figure out what the spell was supposed to be used for. That's all we need to know."

Aaron picked up a cloth and used it to turn the page. He dropped the cloth off to the side and absentmindedly rubbed his fingers on his pants leg as if he had touched something gross and needed to get the feeling off.

The left-hand page was the one Brandon had shown them at the café. The right side was new. It was filled with script and had more oddly colored stains that Yani tried not to think about. Aaron focused on the page he hadn't seen yet. Yani knew he had found something horrible when Aaron's face lost all color. Aaron kept reading, but his hands were shaking. Everyone was focused on that trembling, waiting for Aaron to finish reading the page and tell them what he had found.

Aaron took a stumbling step backward when he reached the end of the page. Yani reached forward to steady him with a gentle hand on his shoulder.

"Djinni," he gasped. "Someone summoned and enslaved an ifrit djinni."

Brandon and Bishop both gasped as if this were something horrible. Yani knew what djinn were, but he was ignorant of the implications. Yakov apparently was too.

"I don't recognize the term," Yakov said.

Bishop answered. "It's Middle Eastern mythology, from pre-Muslim Arabic peoples, although it was eventually adopted into large portions of Islam. A djinni is sometimes called a type of angel, but just as often they're considered to be minions of Satan. Generally, they exist as smoke, but they have unbelievably strong magical powers so could easily appear as some sort of animal or even as a human."

"And an ifrit?" Martin asked. He pressed his lips tightly together after he spoke, as if he didn't like what he was hearing. Yani certainly didn't. Djinn sounded dangerous, and somehow he didn't think one summoned and bound with so much death and blood in the spell was a good thing.

"An ifrit is one of the ones from hell," Aaron said softly. "Their magic is weaker, but that only makes them easier to enslave. Overall, they are very strong, but the most fearsome thing about them is their control over fire." He paused, looking at the book for a long moment as he swallowed heavily. "You really think a hunter"—that he meant his father went unsaid—"performed this spell?"

"There's a certain smell to magic," Bishop explained. "Fresh magic, recently cast, is the easiest to trace. Brandon has the strongest nose of all my grandchildren, but our librarian is a lamia. She can taste magic, and her tongue told her this spell in this book was freshest."

"My nose is telling me the same thing," Brandon insisted. "I smell blood and the tang of magic on these pages specifically."

"So what does this mean?" Yakov asked. He was pressed close to Martin's side, as if just the knowledge was frightening enough that he wanted the comfort and security of his lover. Yani could commiserate—he could use a hug too—but he didn't have a deep relationship with Aaron yet.

Bishop hissed in a breath through his teeth. "Summoned creatures are forced back to their original plane when their summoner dies. It could mean nothing, that the ifrit returned to hell after the hunter's death, but the fact that we didn't see any indication that fire was used in the fighting at the compound leads me to believe someone else summoned the ifrit. The leader had a hand in the spell, but he was not the intended recipient of the ifrit's powers and protection." He grimaced and shook his head. "So most likely this means we're looking for an evil spell caster with an ifrit djinni at his beck and call."

"We should monitor the police radio for unusual fire activity," Brandon said thoughtfully.

"I'll work on a spell to see if we can locate it," Aaron added.

Yani looked around the assembled people and had to suppress a shiver. They were afraid, and that fear propelled them to act before it was too late. Two vampires, two werewolves, an incubus, and a mage all had their heads together to try to stop whatever was going to happen. Yani stood in the middle of their group and wondered why he was being included. Yes, he was Yakov's nephew, and he was in a relationship of sorts with Aaron, but he was otherwise as normal a human as anyone could be. He was just a kid almost finished with an undergraduate degree in international relations; his biggest future plans were to take a gap year to study for his LSATs while working so he could save some money to pay for law school. He didn't know anything about djinn or magic.

These were his friends and family, so of course Yani wanted to support them. Yet, he felt he might do that best by staying out of their way. It wasn't a good feeling in the pit of Yani's stomach, which was churning with worry and acid.

"We didn't find any indication that a spell of this nature was actually performed at the hunter compound," Luke was saying as Yani stepped out of their circle and backed away a few feet. "Was there anywhere your father liked to go that could be used to perform this?"

Aaron was already shaking his head in denial. "I honestly can't think of anything, but I'll look into his bank statements and credit-card records. Maybe I inherited a property I don't know about?"

Yani turned around, unable to even face the group as they spoke. He had nothing to add to the conversation, no insight that could help them figure out who and why and what. He faced the cavernous room with its rows and rows of bookshelves and wished that weren't true. Heck, even the small green lizard sitting on the shelf over by the pile of books from the compound looked like he understood what they were talking about more than Yani.

The lizard was barely the length of Yani's hand and was the shade of pale green only found in creatures like it. Its head was cocked to the side as if it were listening intently. A little green lizard had found its way deep underground, and it wasn't hiding in fear or starving to death?

"Hey, guys," Yani called, interrupting their conversation. He felt a bit stupid for pointing it out—it could just be an ordinary lizard—but something didn't feel right. "We're being watched." All eyes turned to follow Yani's pointing finger.

Martin hissed, his fangs visible and angry. Bishop and Brandon both snarled, an inhuman, animal sound that made Yani's ears ache. Aaron flung out one hand as the lizard spun and made to dive deeper into the shelf.

The lizard froze in place, immobile as Aaron's spell took hold. Bishop stalked over and used one of the protective cloths to turn the lizard around.

"Who do you belong to?" he snarled in the lizard's face, his face contorting slightly so he looked more than just human, as if his face were comprised of both human and wolf bones to Yani's inexperienced eyes.

"One of you has eyes-that-see, but you'll all burn in the end!" The lizard's mouth didn't move, but the voice definitely emanated from near its head. "Burn—I'll see you all burned!"

"So you are the ifrit?" Aaron asked, but his voice held too much skepticism for him to actually believe that the ifrit was in the room with them.

"Oh, no, silly magician. Oh, no, you'll burn second. After the one who has eyes-that-see. Oh yes, after the eyes-that-see is burnt to a crisp."

Magnified

The lizard began to convulse as the voice laughed and laughed, and it suddenly burst into flames. Aaron swore and started chanting in what sounded like Hebrew, although Yani only recognized a few words. The fire flared white-hot, and the smell of burning paper filled the air. Aaron's chanting grew louder as black smoke began to drift ominously in their direction.

As suddenly as the fire had started, it stopped, and Aaron collapsed to his knees. He was panting for breath and shaking slightly. The lizard was entirely reduced to ash, but the smoke had dissipated and not even an ember still smoldered.

"That was a familiar," Brandon snarled. "The ifrit was spying on us for his master."

"At least we have confirmation that the ifrit still exists on this plane," Martin said calmly. He was standing between Yakov and the pile of ash, as if his body could protect Yakov from any harm. "We know at least part of what we're fighting against."

"That's not exactly a comfort," Luke groaned.

No, it really wasn't.

"All of you are going to accept the protection of the coalition," Bishop said. He was frowning, but his face looked wholly human again. He turned and walked back to the spell book still open on the table. He took another cloth, firmly closed the book, and then carried it to the other side of the table where he buried it in the middle of the stacks of books there.

"What does that entail, specifically?" Martin asked. His voice was bland, but Yani thought he still sounded unhappy with the idea.

"A safe bed to sleep in," Bishop replied immediately. He gestured toward the vault door and waited while everyone congregated before walking over and inputting a code on the keypad.

The lights went out without warning, and Yani heard the clunk of the giant bar unlocking. The door slowly inched open, and the sconce lighting in the hall beyond allowed Yani to see where he needed to walk. He was in the middle of the group as they all moved quickly toward the light. The door closed again behind them, and Bishop pushed past until he led the way up the stairs.

"This house is warded with three generations of spells imbedded into the stones as they were built. Neither an ifrit nor his master could easily enter, whereas your home in New York or your dorms and apartments in Boston will burn with you already dead inside."

They were silent for a few minutes as they climbed. Yani felt exhausted, as if the entire day had dragged even if it had only been caused by the last hour. They reached the landing and turned the corner to continue up the stairs.

"Yakov and I will return before sunrise," Martin said finally.

"I will have a bed ready for you," Bishop replied, fully understanding the sacrifice they were making. Vampires were helpless during the day, and allowing someone else to ensure their security took a lot of trust.

"Some of us have class during the day," Luke grumbled. Yani agreed with him. He couldn't afford to miss class. He still had a month before finals, and if he stopped attending class, he would flunk them all, which was unacceptable.

They walked up a few more stairs before Bishop answered. "School is too important. Brandon and Aaron can take care of themselves in an emergency. Luke, how strong are your powers?"

Luke snorted. "I can entice anyone I want, male or female, young or old. But that doesn't matter, because I can escape to the dream plane if there's an emergency."

Yani couldn't see well in the dim light, but he thought Bishop shot Luke an impressed look over his shoulder. Yani already knew where the conversation was going and he wasn't impressed. With himself, mostly. It was the same argument he had been having down in that evil library. He didn't belong, and he was definitely the weakest link in their group. It wasn't a nice feeling.

"Someone needs to be with Yani twenty-four seven," Aaron insisted. He sounded worried, and Yani felt one of his hands groping the air behind him until Yani gave in and placed his hand in Aaron's.

Yani couldn't say no. His life was in danger, so of course he would be staying at the coalition house. Yet something didn't quite sit right.

"If the spells on this building are so strong, how did the lizard get in?" Yani asked. It was a legitimate concern, given that Bishop was offering them a safe haven that might not actually be safe.

Bishop snorted in disgust to himself. "Familiars interact oddly with magic, particularly wards. They register as animals instead of magical creatures and are able to slip by where others can't. However—" He paused and threw a grin over his shoulder. "—now that we're forewarned, those of us with good noses will be able to pick them out. I'll have the house searched before dawn and increase patrols."

Yani's legs were feeling shaky, but he continued doggedly up the stairs. No one else appeared to be having any problems, but then no one else was a mere human. He tried to push his feelings of inadequacy away, but they were pervasive. He felt weighed down, which didn't help him keep up with the others.

Aaron fell back with Yani. He wasn't winded at all. Yani didn't know if that was because he was in great shape or if his magic gave him a little more stamina. It did make him feel slightly jealous though it also gave him an idea.

"Could you teach me magic?" he asked softly.

Aaron paused for a second on the stairs as he stared at Yani in surprise. "I'm not sure," he replied slowly. "You have to have an affinity for it, but it usually manifests with puberty if you do."

"Oh," Yani sighed, his shoulders drooping in defeat.

"But even if I can't teach you, I'm sure there's someone in the coalition who can," Aaron hurried to add. "Even if it's just how to throw a punch, that's better than nothing, right?"

"Right," Yani agreed resolutely. Whatever he could learn had to be better than what he had at the moment, which was nothing.

They reached the end of the stairs and a blank wall. Bishop did something to the wall, and Yani could see another keypad slide into view over everyone's shoulders. Bishop input a code, and the door clicked open at the same time as the stairway lights went off. The light filtering through from behind the door replaced the sconce lighting, and it grew as Bishop pushed the door open. Yani followed the group as they filed through the door and stepped out into a kitchen.

The kitchen was full of stainless-steel appliances and marble countertops. It looked top of the line to Yani's admittedly inexperienced eyes, and it wasn't even close to the sitting room they had originally entered the staircase from. There hadn't been any turns or any other doorways that would lead them to a different destination, yet somehow that had happened anyway. Yani decided it was probably better not to ask how. Someone would probably just shrug unhelpfully and explain that it was magic.

"I will call a car so everyone can go and get their things," Bishop said once everyone had entered the kitchen and the door was firmly closed behind them. Yani couldn't even see where the door had been.

Aaron and Brandon got into the car with Yani, but Luke, Uncle Yakov, and Uncle Martin waved off the offer of transportation. They drove back to the city in silence.

They had been living in their little house for long enough that they had started to accumulate stuff. A few weeks ago, they spent a nice night walking along the boardwalk in New Jersey; the stuffed souvenir from one of the games Yakov had played sat on the couch in their living room. Much of the house displayed similar lived-in qualities. The place was more like a home than a safe place to rest their heads during the day ought to be. They had clearly spent far too much time living in the US.

Martin found himself missing their quiet manor in Poland where the townspeople cowered in superstitious awe of the lord they had never seen. Martin was a hermit to them, although every fifty to seventy years he contacted the local newspaper to announce his death and that his successor had taken up residence in the manor in order to allay some of their fears.

Yakov had located a bag and was busy carefully folding their clothes into it.

"We could leave now, beloved," Martin said softly, aware that Yakov's hands were shaking slightly as he clutched the cloth of one of Martin's shirts. "We could return home and be safe from the ifrit djinni. We do not have to get any more involved."

Yakov looked up from his folding, his eyes blazing with indignation. "We are already involved. The coalition is relying on your experience as a master, as is the vampire coven whose own master is still missing. Yani is relying on me to help keep everyone safe, and if I abandon him like that, I would never forgive myself."

Yakov's hands steadied on the shirt as he spoke. His voice had been strengthened with conviction. Martin smiled slightly and rested his own hands over Yakov's. He bent down to claim a chaste kiss.

"Good," Marin said softly before kissing Yakov again. "We should hurry with our packing so we can feed and be back at the coalition building before dawn."

Yakov gaped as Martin drew away to go find a second bag for their belongings. He glanced down at his steady hands and shut his mouth with a snap.

"Conniving bastard," he grumbled under his breath after Martin's abrupt change, no doubt perfectly aware that Martin could hear him. Yakov was smiling, though, so Martin knew everything would be okay.

Four:Dreams

Myobu Sensei was a tiny Japanese woman. She wore her long black hair tied tightly on the top of her head, which emphasized her traditional yukata and the three fox tails waving lazily behind her. She was an inari kitsune, but Yani didn't think it was just her supernatural abilities that made her as fast and strong as she was.

Bishop introduced her to Yani a week ago, after Aaron wasn't able to teach him to light a candle with magic. Yani very quickly learned he didn't have any magical abilities whatsoever; he was a typical human. Yet, humans were still able to do great things with just their bodies. Sensei had tucked his thumb around his fist, pointed him toward a punching bag in a large exercise room in the coalition building, and let him punch. Every once in a while, she would whack his elbow with the bamboo sword she carried at her waist to correct his form, but otherwise she just watched as Yani alternated hands and punched.

He didn't think she spoke any English, but that didn't stop her from communicating that she was generally displeased with his minimal progress. Jews played tennis or mahjong, not contact sports. They weren't generally known for their athleticism, including punching. Their brains had sustained Jews during the many centuries when the only employment Jews were allowed to take up were as merchants or moneylenders. Both were positions that required high levels of math and reading. Jews had been banned from being carpenters or blacksmiths, or any other high-sweat employment, for hundreds of years. It had actually been against the law in most of Europe. That had changed, of course, after the Holocaust when only the strongest and most resilient Jews had been able to survive the cruelty of the Nazis. It was why the Israeli army was the strongest in the world. The US sent their Marines to train in Israel because of that.

But just because his family had survived the Holocaust didn't mean Yani's genes had been magically changed to make him brawny and strong. Besides, his dad's side of the family had moved to the US in the 1800s, missing the Holocaust by a few decades when they fled from England and the Anglican Church's insistence that they convert or leave. Either way, Yani would never have the muscles needed to be a true master of the art he was learning.

He was learning how to punch, though. Slowly and surely.

At the end of the lesson, Sensei tapped him on the shoulder with her katana to indicate she was done with him and left the gym. Yani dropped his aching arms and went to find water.

Aaron was waiting for him next to the water fountain. He stood silently as Yani gratefully gulped down water and handed over a towel for Yani to wipe his face when he was done.

"We should… Could we talk?" Aaron asked awkwardly. Since their brief stint of handholding two weeks ago, they had barely had a moment to sit near each other. Bishop and another mage had been present when Aaron was testing Yani for magic, so that hadn't been a good time, and they had been shuttled to and from classes separately ever since. When they weren't in class, Yani was punching things and Aaron was studying ancient books to try to figure out how to banish a djinni.

"Yes," Yani replied eagerly. He wanted to know just what that moment of holding hands meant to Aaron, if it meant the same to him as it did to Yani, and if there might be something more to their relationship than just that. "Let's go find somewhere more private."

Their bedroom was out. A shared space with six beds kept clean and ready for whoever needed a place to sleep at night, the room was never empty.

"One of the practice rooms should be free," Aaron said. The practice rooms were specially shielded rooms for mages and other magical creatures to practice their craft without destroying the entire building by accident. Yani followed Aaron down the hallway until he found an empty room. They took seats across the small table in the middle of the room.

Yani didn't know how to start their conversation, and he suspected Aaron didn't either as they sat in awkward silence for a few very long minutes. One of them had to speak eventually, and Yani finally decided it might as well be him.

The words came out so quickly Yani barely understood himself. He felt like he had to get everything out in one rapid swoop or he might lose the opportunity. Yani didn't want yet another two weeks to go by before they had another chance to try to figure their relationship out. "Do you like me? I like you, and I'd like to try dating once all this craziness with the djinni is over."

Aaron nodded immediately after Yani finally shut his mouth again. "I do like you, and that sounds like a great idea to me." His voice was also rushed, as if he was as worried about missing out on something potentially great between them if they didn't get on the same page now. A small smile flitted across his face and stayed there as he held one hand across the table for Yani to take. Aaron's hand was slightly clammy with nervous sweat, but Yani didn't mind because his fingers were also warm and his grip tight and comforting.

This was everything his last relationship wasn't, which was marvelous. Aaron was soft and gentle, but they didn't lack in the least for sexual tension. Above their clasped hands, their eyes met, and the instant heat that frizzled between them tightened something low in Yani's gut. He'd never felt this way before, but it was certainly welcome.

Yani licked his lips involuntarily. He felt a little like he was under Luke's spell, pulled in to Aaron's eyes and body without thought of refusal. There wasn't any coercion magic involved though, just feelings and genuine want. Aaron tilted his head first and leaned forward, but Yani was barely a beat behind. Their lips met softly. The table between their bodies kept them separated. Still, the feel of Aaron's lips, soft and pliant underneath Yani's, sent a shivering thrill down Yani's spine. He groaned and tried to press closer, forgetting that there was a table between them in his eagerness.

Aaron slowly drew away. Yani wanted to reach out and yank him close again, to tangle their tongues together and start losing some clothing. Admittedly, it had been a while since Yani had sex, and his body was scolding him for that lack. His brain was more on board with what his body was aching for than was probably entirely healthy. That Aaron was the one holding Yani close only electrified the experience even more.

"There's someone at the door," Aaron explained after taking a moment to catch his breath.

Magnified

That got Yani's brain to start functioning properly again. He ran a hand through his hair, as if the motion could force back his libido and allow rational thought back into control. Yani turned his head and saw Orath, the man who drove him to and from school, peeking through the tiny window in the door. Yani didn't know what species Orath belonged to, but when he smiled, like he was doing at the moment, a lot of extra, pointy teeth appeared.

"I have class in a half hour," Yani groaned, disappointed in himself that he had forgotten in the rush and excitement of figuring out what was going on between him and Aaron. Aaron laughed, which made Yani laugh too. They would never have free time to explore their relationship in private. Yani wasn't just thinking about sex, although that part would be nice too. He wanted to go on a real date with Aaron without the weight of everything else hovering over them the entire time.

Aaron leaned forward to peck Yani on the lips quickly before resolutely turning to the door. He opened it and stepped outside. Yani followed, but stopped to speak with Orath while Aaron continued down the hall.

"You want to skip class today?" Orath asked with a very wide grin. His accent sounded Scandinavian, but for some strange reason Yani couldn't help thinking it was Scandinavian that actually sounded like Orath.

"I can't," Yani sighed wistfully. "I'm going to go grab my bag. I'll meet you by the front door?"

Orath's pointed grin didn't abate in the slightest as he nodded and turned to head down the hall toward the front door. Yani hurried in the other direction, climbing a back staircase until he reached the correct floor. Mimsy was floating serenely above his or her bed, sleeping. Yani didn't know which gender Mimsy was or even if Mimsy had a gender. Not that it mattered to Yani, who was more focused on finding a clean shirt and stuffing his computer into his bag in record time. Yani hurried back out of the room and headed to where Orath was waiting.

As long as they didn't hit any Boston traffic—an impossibility—Yani would make it to class on time. He was probably going to be late, but the professor didn't take attendance until midway through the class so it should be okay.

"Yani! There you are! I've been looking everywhere for you!" Rachel latched onto his arm and gripped tightly. He could feel every contour of her boobs thanks to the way she was pressing his hand against her chest, and it made his skin crawl.

Yani tried to unsuccessfully tug his arm free. "Hello, Rachel," he groaned. There had to be a way to get away from her. He was just supposed to meet Brandon for a quick dinner in the dining hall before their ride came. Rachel must have been staking out the dining hall to catch him so quickly and ruthlessly.

"I told you to call me Chava!" she insisted. "I could really use some help with that paper," she added leadingly. She also squeezed Yani's hand tightly, forcing his fingers to close indecently around her breast.

Yani had enough. He forcibly yanked his hand free from hers and turned on her with a glare. "I have a boyfriend, Rachel. Please stop coming on to me, and write your own damned paper for once in your life." He stomped away, hoping she wouldn't follow to try yet again. He grabbed a quick burger and fries from the grill station, got a glass of juice, and collapsed into a chair across from Ettie.

Magnified

"Is she a blind succubus or something?" he grumbled cruelly.

Ettie looked up from her pudding cup and shrugged. "Just a dumbass, I think. I'm going to get some more. You want some?"

"No, thanks," Yani sighed. One hamburger was bad enough. If he ate a pudding and Sensei found out, he would be doing punches until his arms actually fell off. She had sighed one too many times about the little extra layer of chub around his middle, by which Sensei meant he didn't have any sign of a six-pack. He was still very thin, just not muscled.

Brandon dropped his tray in front of the seat next to Yani before pulling out the chair and sitting down. "That Rachel girl is going to get arrested at some point, mark my words." He was laughing at Yani's sour face, but at least he was trying to be a good friend. Yani stuffed his mouth with burger so he wouldn't have to reply.

"Is Miss Chava really so droll?" a voice Yani didn't recognize asked from just behind them. A boy Yani didn't know circled the table and sat down directly across from him. His hair was a brilliant shade of red—it had to be dyed that color—and his skin was very black. Except the color wasn't the natural black of skin. Instead it looked like the black of charcoal. "Hmm, eyes-that-see? Is Miss Chava such a bad person?"

The boy looked up, and Yani saw his eyes were flickering red, as if a candle flame had replaced his iris.

"She's pretty damned obnoxious, that's for sure," Brandon joked, as if the boy sitting across the table wasn't scary as hell. Yani clasped one hand tightly around Brandon's forearm to get him to shut up, his nails probably digging in a little too forcefully.

"How do you know Rachel?" Yani asked carefully, wondering if there was actually a way to get out of this alive.

"Call her Chava!" the creature snarled. Fire licked around his teeth, which no longer looked human to Yani's eyes. They were pointed and spaced like a wolf's. His face was elongating too, losing its rounded shape as the nose turned into a pointed beak.

"Yani, what?" Brandon began, but Yani dug his nails in again and Brandon shut up.

"Ifrit," Yani said in reply, hoping his heart wasn't about to beat right out of his chest, "what are you doing here?"

"Call me Ifrit. Call me Flame. Call me Pain. Call me Death. You will all burn in the end!" His voice was booming, but no one else in the dining hall was turning to look at the commotion. Only Yani could see and hear the real him.

"Not today, demon," Luke snarled in return. Yani and Brandon both jumped in surprise when Luke's hands landed on their shoulders. There was a yanking feeling in Yani's gut, as if he were being pulled backward, and his chair was tipping uncontrollably. The dining hall wavered in front of his eyes, the ifrit snarling and reaching out one hand as if he could catch Yani before his head hit the floor.

And then, suddenly, Yani wasn't in the dining hall any longer. The familiar room vanished as if Yani had blinked and the movie he was watching had changed scenes. Except the movie was his life.

Yani was in a sitting position, but there was no longer a chair underneath his butt. Gravity took hold, and he fell to the floor with a thump. His feet were tangled in his bag, so Yani had to straighten that out before he could think about standing again. He tossed his bag over his shoulder when he had it untangled and looked around curiously.

Magnified

"Oh, you stupid, stupid puppy," Luke was gasping. His body was wrapped around Brandon's, and he was shaking as he murmured into Brandon's ear. Aside from his friends, Yani couldn't actually see anything. The surroundings were gray from the ground to the sky. There wasn't any grass or other objects to break up the constant monotony, just endless gray. The gray itself seemed to be shifting as if it were water pulled along by a current.

"Where are we?" Yani asked at the same time Brandon pulled away from Luke and asked, "Why are you both acting so weird?"

Brandon looked around for another second while both Yani and Luke gaped at him incredulously. "Where'd that guy go? Why are you sitting on the floor, Yani?"

"You are such a stupid puppy," Luke sighed. He turned to look at Yani. "Eyes-that-see, huh? That explains a lot. Brandon, tell me what you see right now."

"Okay? I mean we're still in the dining hall. There's not really much to see."

"What do you see, Yani?"

"Gray," Yani answered immediately. "Shifting gray currents. Where are we?"

Luke smiled grimly at Yani. "We are on the dream plane, where illusion and dreams meet. But your eyes apparently don't see illusion. You saw right through the ifrit's human disguise, and you're seeing the dream plane as an incubus might instead of a human."

"What does that mean?" Yani asked. He touched the corner of one eye, as if he could find the answer there.

"It means you're not as much of a magic null as we originally thought. Now, get to your feet. We've got to hurry before everyone at the coalition learns we've gone missing and runs into the ifrit while they're searching for us."

Yani scrambled to his feet and moved closer to Luke. The ground felt almost spongy beneath his feet, as if he were walking on a shifting cloud.

Luke seemed to know which direction to walk in. He led the way through the gray, and Yani made certain to stay close. Brandon kept flinching every once in a while as they walked, which was hilarious to watch.

"I'm literally walking through walls here, guys," he explained when he caught them grinning at him. "I swear, if the next one is solid and I break my nose, I'm going to be pissed."

"Try not to bleed here," Luke replied, his smile unabated.

They walked for a few more minutes in silence, the gray continuing to swirl creepily around them. It was so damned weird, and the constant silence made it worse. The continually shifting scenery around them made him think he should be hearing waves or a breeze. He couldn't even hear his own footsteps, let alone a more natural noise. Yani cracked and spoke, unable to handle it any longer.

"How far are we going to walk in the dream plane?" he asked Luke.

"You and Brandon are going all the way to the coalition building. It was easy enough for me to drag you both into dreams, since you've both been my prey for so long—"

"What?" Brandon interrupted.

Luke's grin turned salacious. "You're my favorite prey," he said, his voice low and sultry. He reached out to run one finger down Brandon's cheek, and then his other hand reached between Brandon's legs and got a good grip. Brandon let out a low moan. Yani rolled his eyes and turned his back on the show. "You're also my last prey, the one I'll feed off for the rest of my life." Yani heard the pop and squelch of kissing behind him. It didn't last too long, and now that Yani had the start of something with Aaron, he didn't feel too jealous.

Luke cleared his throat and touched Yani on the shoulder to indicate they were moving on.

"Anyway, since I've fed off both of you multiple times, I could pull you into the dream plane, but it's not designed to allow prey to leave again once they're caught. Luckily, the coalition has a doorway that spans planes, so I can force you out through there."

"Forcing doesn't sound like fun," Brandon said in a worried echo of Yani's thoughts.

"Nah, I'll pop out of the dream plane to tell them to have the door already open. You'll just walk through."

The silence of the dream plane didn't feel as oppressive now that Yani knew they would be reaching the end at some point. It still gave him the willies, though, and he couldn't wait until he was back in the real world again. Eventually, a gray smudge in the distance began to resolve itself as a separate entity inside the plane. It was a slightly darker color than the rest of the surroundings, and as Yani slowly drew closer, he saw that it also had a fixed outline unlike everything else around him.

It was a door, hazy and indistinct, but definitely a door.

"Sit down and rest for a moment," Luke said once they reached the door. "Let me hop on over and get them to open the door on their side." He vanished in midair a second later. Yani gratefully took Luke's advice, sitting down on the spongy ground with relief. His legs ached, and his bag felt far too heavy for only holding a textbook and his computer.

Since there wasn't anything else to look at, Yani studied the door. There was a handle exactly where one should be on a door, but no jamb or even a wall to support it. The door was planted directly into the ground, and that was apparently enough to keep it from tipping over.

The door suddenly grew even hazier, as if a cloud had passed between it and Yani. He reached up to rub his eyes, but when he brought his hands down, the door was gone. The gray was gone too. Instead, he was standing at the side of a rumbling train track. A little imp, a type of supernatural creature the size and shape of a rabbit that liked mischief and mayhem, was busy rusting out a length of the track. Before he could complete his task, a bird of prey screeched overhead and the imp dove for cover. The train roared past, its wheels clicking and clacking harmlessly over the abused bit of track.

The scene changed, the tracks fading away to be replaced by a new image. This time, Yani recognized what he was seeing. He hadn't ever had the opportunity to travel around Eastern Europe and visit any concentration camps, but it was on his bucket list. The pictures from history books hardly did the scene around him justice, but they had certainly tried.

Yani didn't know which camp he was looking at, but he was standing in the middle of a long line. The people around him were emaciated to the point that they looked like walking skeletons, their threadbare clothes hanging off their bodies. Just in front of Yani was a man so thin that his arms were shaking as he held an infant child to his chest. The man looked up, and suddenly Yani knew exactly what he himself would look like if he lost fifty or sixty pounds of fat and muscle. Except he wasn't looking at a mirror image of himself. He was looking at Yakov standing in the horrible line, Shimon in his arms. Next to him was Gramma Chana and her four children. Aryeh, the child who hadn't survived, was alive and clutching Chana's skirts. Gideon, Shmuley, and Aharon were standing nearby. Yani didn't know how he was able to recognize them all when they were so young and tortured-looking, but he somehow knew exactly what he was seeing.

Magnified

The line slowly moved forward. Yani's feet never moved—rather, the scene moved around him without noticing his presence. He slowly approached a man wearing a smartly pressed SS uniform and watched as Yakov was sent to the right and Chana and the children to the left. Yakov didn't even have a chance to say goodbye as Shimon was pulled from his arms and pressed into Chana's instead.

Chana was sent to the showers, and Yani watched as his family suffered and died horrifically from Zyklon B poisoning. Their bodies were tossed onto a cart that eventually led to the fire. Yani didn't know what had eventually happened to Yakov, and apparently it wasn't important for the vision. The scene dissolved around him, whirling with colors and sounds as time whizzed past. Eventually, it resolved itself again.

Yani had only been inside the hunters' compound twice, but he would never be able to forget any detail from those horrible times. He was in the middle of another battle. Guns were being fired, and that damned crossbow twanged repeatedly. The hunters weren't fighting vampires this time. No, they were fighting werewolves and other creatures; people Yani knew from his time with the coalition. Bishop was there, and so was Brandon. Luke was absent, and Yani didn't see himself anywhere. Although, if Grandpa Gideon had died in the Holocaust, then Yani didn't exist. He hadn't been confined in the hunters' execution grounds and awoken the dead vampires. Instead, the coalition had acted against the hunters in order to stop them killing vampires arbitrarily. Aaron was fighting, but he was fighting on the side of his father. He and Brandon were enemies and someone was going to die horribly. Yani could feel it deep in the marrow of his bones.

"Yani, wake up!"

The fighting was getting bloodier. Wolves were transforming from their human shape and guns were being reloaded with fresh clips. The crossbow's accuracy only seemed to get even better with each shot fired.

The scene was shaking and Yani's cheek was stinging. Had he been shot? Or was the scene dissolving again? Somehow, Yani didn't think the scene would dissolve until after he saw his friends die.

"Yani! Come on!"

Yani blinked. He could still see the fighting, but a funny sort of gray matter overlaid it. He blinked again, and the gray asserted itself. The hunters' compound faded away as if it had never been there.

"What happened?" Yani asked. His voice sounded croaky, as if he had been crying, and when he brought a shaking hand up to check, he found tears drying on his face.

Luke breathed out a sigh of relief. His hands were on Yani's shoulders; he had been shaking Yani to try to wake him, which was why the scene had gone so wonky.

"You were caught by a nightmare," Luke explained. "I removed it, but the poison doesn't fade until you wake up again…if you wake up again."

"You just started sobbing," Brandon gasped, looking wide-eyed at both Yani and the gray dream plane around them, as if he could stop another nightmare before it pounced.

Yani dried his face on his sleeve. "Can we get out of here now?" he asked plaintively. He'd had enough of ifrits and dream planes for the day. He really, really had.

Luke's worried frown turned into a small smile. "The door's open on the other side. They'd just gotten confirmation that you weren't at the pickup point from Brandon's uncle Ben. I showed up just in time to stop a search party from forming."

He got his hands underneath Yani's armpits and levered Yani to his feet. Yani took two staggering steps before he got his feet underneath him properly. He was grateful that Luke didn't take his stabilizing hand off of Yani's arm. Luke steered them in the direction of the door. He reached out and turned the knob, pushing the door open slowly. As soon as the door was open, he took a stronger grip on Yani's arm and literally threw him through the doorway. Yani hit the open door and felt the slightest resistance. Whatever he felt couldn't stand up to his momentum, and he went flying through.

Yani got his hands up just in time to catch himself before he crashed into a wall. He stumbled to the side as Brandon was also tossed through the door. Brandon wasn't as lucky with his hands, hitting the wall face-first with a splat. Luke calmly stepped through the door and closed it carefully behind him.

They were standing on a small landing. There was a staircase leading down and a staircase leading up. Small sconces on the wall were lit to illuminate the space. They were standing in the staircase that led to the evil library, Yani realized. His legs felt even more exhausted than the last time he'd needed to climb the stairs, but he resolutely put one foot in front of the other as he began to climb. Brandon was groaning and grumping about hitting the wall to an unsympathetic Luke behind Yani as they joined him on the stairs.

Yani couldn't guess how much time he had spent inside the dream plane or how long it took to climb the stairs. His legs were numb, but his feet screamed in pain every time he put his foot down on another step. Slowly, painfully, he made his way upward.

The door at the top of the stairs was closed, but it was such a welcome sight that Yani let out an involuntary gasp of relief. Luke reached past Yani to knock on the door.

There was a *thunk*, and the sconce lighting abruptly turned off. The stairs were unbelievably dark, but that was welcome too after the constant and unending gray. The door creaked as it was pushed open.

Bishop opened the door. Lara stood behind him, a first-aid kit clutched to her chest. Just behind her was Aaron. Yani's legs somehow propelled him through the door, past Lara, and into Aaron's waiting arms.

"Is anyone hurt?" Lara asked immediately before anyone could say anything else.

Yani didn't answer. Aaron's arms were strong and warm around Yani—exactly what he needed at the moment. He was holding up most of Yani's weight too.

"I think we'll need some painkillers from all the walking we had to do," Luke explained for them all. "Otherwise we're uninjured."

Yani heard another *thunk* as the door closed. He let himself be manhandled into the soft cushions of a nearby couch. Aaron's arm settled over Yani's shoulders, and Yani leaned gratefully into Aaron's body.

"Tell me what happened," Bishop insisted.

Yani peeled his eyes open, fighting back his exhaustion in order to pay attention to Bishop. They were sitting in a comfortable living room, totally different from every other room he had ever entered or exited the staircase from.

"I don't know how it started exactly," Luke began. He was sitting in a cozy armchair with Brandon on his lap. It looked like Brandon had already fallen asleep. There was a little smudge of blood under his nose, but otherwise he looked unmarred by the journey. "When I got there, Yani was staring down the ifrit djinni. Brandon had no idea what was happening. He couldn't see it, but Yani could, and he spoke with it."

"What did it say?" Bishop asked immediately, his focus switching from Luke to Yani. He was sitting on a long couch, Lara at his side looking concerned.

Magnified

"It repeated what Rachel had been telling me. Asked me why I wouldn't call her Chava." Yani's words were slightly slurred with exhaustion, but Bishop understood him anyway.

"Who is Rachel?"

"Her name's Rachel Anders," Yani explained, trying to force his brain into dredging up the proper information. "She gets through school by sleeping with anyone who will then give her a hand with her homework. She picked me as her next target so she could pass the class we're both taking."

"And the djinni defended her in front of you?" Bishop asked curiously. "I will have a quick look into Rachel Anders. Maybe she'll provide a clue. In the meantime, get some rest. I will speak with Myobu Sensei about postponing your lesson tomorrow."

Yani's eyes slid closed again, sleep quickly creeping up on him. The memory of Chana's horrified face as no water was released as she turned the taps in those terrible Nazi showers popped up. Yani's eyes opened again.

Bishop and Lara were gone, but Luke and Brandon hadn't moved. "Will I dream?" he asked Luke.

Luke grimaced unhappily. "If you do dream, it won't be the ones from the dream plane. The nightmare ate those. You'll remember them when you're awake, but they won't ever plague your sleep again."

Yani nodded and his eyes slid closed again. With Luke's assurances fresh in his mind and Aaron's warm chest under his cheek, Yani fell asleep quickly.

Yani's legs were columns of agony when he finally woke up again. He was tucked in bed, the blankets pulled up to his chin. He had been only half-awake a moment ago, drifting in the peace of nonawareness, when he attempted to roll onto his side to get more comfortable. Pain cramped his muscles the second his legs shifted, and he couldn't help the involuntary scream that erupted.

He lived in Boston and walked everywhere! His legs shouldn't hurt so badly just from a little walking. His feet, sure, but not the rest. Yet, agony was too kind a word to use to describe how bad he was feeling. His hips and knees were burning as if a fire had been lit in the joints. The muscles felt like white-hot needles were buried deep in his flesh and were moving around.

"It's the dream plane," Luke said softly, as if he thought just the sound of his voice could distract Yani. He was so very wrong. His hand was rubbing gentle circles on Yani's back as Yani gasped for breath and tried not to move. Brandon hovered at Luke's side, as if he was unsure how to help. "We walked the distance between your campus and the coalition in a third of the time and distance, but the dream plane made your body think the effort required was quadruple what the longer walk in the human plane would have taken. Aaron ran to find the healer," Luke finished soothingly.

Yani just wanted the pain to stop. One leg was jerking with almost constant spasms and the other just shaking uncontrollably. Every shift exacerbated the pain, yet he couldn't stop the involuntary muscle tremors. His muscles had to move to relieve something, Yani didn't have the medical knowhow to understand what, but every movement also lit off another fresh bout of agony.

The bedroom door opened, and Yani heard footsteps rushing to his side. "Oh my god, Yani!" Aaron gasped. Yani glanced up through tears, his teeth gritted to keep from screaming. Aaron's mouth was pressed tightly closed, his hands hovering ineffectually over Yani as if he didn't know what was safe to touch.

Magnified

"Move out of the way, idiot," a baritone voice insisted. Yani couldn't see who spoke, but a second later a pair of gnarled, hairy hands gripped the blanket covering him and yanked it down the bed. Yani was only in his boxers, which meant someone had stripped him in his sleep. His legs were bent in different directions on the sheet, still twitching and jumping uncontrollably. Yani just wanted it all to end!

The baritone voice grumbled to itself, and then those hairy hands clamped down on Yani's thighs. Yani let out a scream, the touch setting off a new level of agony as if those needles were going to explosively punch through his skin. Seconds later, the pain started to fade. A cool, tingly feeling emanated from those hands, spreading relief. The coolness traveled from his hips, through his thighs, down his calves, and through his feet until even his pinky toes were tingling lightly. The pain was blissfully gone. Yani relaxed into his pillow with a loud groan.

He had thought he would never use his legs again. Yani had actually started hoping someone would save him from the pain by cutting them off entirely. Instead, he felt so much better.

The hands left his legs, but the cool feeling remained behind.

"Don't leave that bed for twenty-four hours," that deep voice instructed. Yani rolled over and sat up slightly so he could look at his savior. The man was maybe three or four feet tall. The brown hair on top of his head was long and unkempt, the curls melding seamlessly with his equally long and messy beard. "You tore some of the muscles and ligaments, which will take a while to properly heal even with my help." His brown eyes were barely visible underneath all the hair and they were crinkled with wrinkles, but they still looked kind.

"Thank you," Yani breathed, glad for anything that could take the pain away.

"I'll be back tonight to see how you're healing," the man continued gruffly before abruptly turning on his heel and walking out of the room.

Aaron held a tissue out. Yani took it and gratefully wiped his face clean of tears and snot. He felt clammy and generally nasty, but without the pain, he didn't honestly care. Of course, looking as unpleasant as he no doubt did in front of Aaron wasn't a plus. "That was awful," he said in a massive understatement.

"I didn't even think how the dream plane would affect a human," Luke said, sounding extremely apologetic. His face was tight with remorse, and his hands were clasped at his chest. Yani, used to Luke's ever cheerful and salacious normality, had never seen Luke look so contrite. "I'm a creature of the dream plane, so it doesn't affect me, and Brandon has werewolf healing. It never even occurred to me that you might experience some side effects. I am so, so sorry, Yani."

"It's…" Yani coughed to clear his throat. It was full of phlegm and scratchy from screaming. "It's okay. The healer helped." The cool, tingly feeling hadn't dissipated, but at the same time his legs felt heavy and unwieldy. Even without the admonition to stay in bed, Yani didn't think he would have taken the chance of walking. The memory of the pain was far too fresh, and his legs felt like tree trunks.

Luke looked unconvinced and continued to hover at Yani's bedside. He had proven to be a good friend, now that he wasn't taking every opportunity to get into Yani's pants, but the mamma-bear routine was getting old. Either Luke needed to sit down and start a conversation or he needed to find some other way to calm down. Aaron was also hovering, although it felt different to Yani. Aaron wasn't feeling guilty, so that weight was absent, but he was also a much more welcome presence. Yani wanted Aaron to hover, except it was still hovering and annoying. If Aaron were to sit, it would be better.

Magnified

Yani had to do something to stop all the hovering before Brandon joined in too, or he'd lose it and snarl at his friends.

"So, I apparently have eyes-that-see?" Yani asked, coming up with a different topic.

Aaron seemed to be glad of the change. He grinned and immediately sat on the edge of the nearest bed. "We're assuming it means you can see through illusion. The ifrit was disguised as a regular human to Brandon's eyes, but you saw through it. The same with the dream plane, which contains a giant illusion meant to calm their prey until it's too late. Basically, spells and entities that are meant to obscure the way something looks don't affect your eyes." He paused and cast around for something, eventually picking up a pencil sticking out of Yani's school bag on the floor. "Tell me when you see a snake," he explained, turning to include Luke and Brandon in the conversation. Aaron mumbled a few words under his breath too quickly for Yani to make them out. The pencil remained unchanged, but Luke let out a little gasp.

"I see it," Luke said. Brandon nodded in agreement. He rested his hands on Luke's shoulders and gently pulled him back until Luke was pressed into his chest. Luke wrapped his arms around Brandon's waist in a natural gesture while still focusing on the pencil in Aaron's hand.

At least the hovering was finished for the moment. Aaron mumbled again and again, checking with Yani each time before he added some magic that Yani assumed was supposed to make the illusion stronger. Aaron was sweating and lightly red in the face by the time Yani thought he saw a slight flicker around the pencil. Aaron mumbled again and Yani gasped.

"It's a garden snake, green with a red stripe down the middle," he said, although the small snake was just a shivery image juxtaposed on top of the yellow number two pencil. "I can still see the pencil, but I also see a projected image on top of it." Aaron mumbled again, but the image didn't change. He was sweating profusely now and panting for breath. He mumbled again, and the pencil started shaking with his hand. The image of the snake obligingly began to shake as well, but it didn't become any stronger.

With a last gasp, Aaron let the spell drop. The snake faded away.

"That's the strongest I can make it," he explained through his gasps as he worked to catch his breath again. "I'd say there aren't many illusions Yani wouldn't be able to see through."

"He bested the power of the dream plane, so that does not surprise me to learn," Bishop said from the doorway. They all jumped in surprise. Yani hadn't known Bishop was in the door, and apparently no one else had either. "I heard you were having a rough morning, Yani. I'm gratified to see that Gem'ma was able to help."

"So he's not just a regular human," Luke said with a wide grin, looking over Brandon's shoulder toward Bishop as he spoke. It stung a little to hear himself called a "regular human" as if there wasn't anything special about being human. But then, the only special thing about being human was the fact that humans were powerless in comparison to the rest of the creatures he had encountered. Yani didn't think there was anything bad about being human, but at the same time he felt a jolt of relief. He had eyes-that-see, which meant he did have something special.

Yani thought back to when they were in the basement library looking at that book of evil spells, and he remembered how much of an outsider he had felt like. Those terrible feelings of inadequacy were gone now. He might not have the healing ability of a werewolf, the enchantment ability of an incubus, or the spells of a mage, but Yani had something and it made him feel good.

"He was never a regular human if he could call on Martin for help," Bishop disagreed. "Having a master vampire for an uncle meant he was part of our world long before he met us."

It was more affirmation for Yani's ego, and it felt good, but that connection was thanks to Uncle Yakov rather than anything Yani had done. His eyes-that-see were much more impressive to him.

Yani arranged the pillows against his headboard and then used his arms to hoist his body higher so he was sitting comfortably upright. His legs were unchanged, which was a relief.

"So, what now?" Yani asked.

Bishop walked farther into the room. He didn't pull up a chair, instead standing next to Brandon and Luke. "We've done some looking in on your friend Rachel. She was a fairly ordinary child from a poor family growing up. No money or plans for college, and she didn't have the academics or athletic ability for a scholarship either. She had a place working in her father's body shop, but her stepmother insisted she at least apply somewhere. Rachel received rejections from every school except yours, Yani, which immediately sent up red flags. Why would she be rejected from less prestigious schools and accepted to one of the best in the city with a full scholarship? Further investigation showed that she has so far passed every single class with an A average, when she couldn't scrape a C in high school."

Rachel could have gotten lucky with one school and decided to turn her life around, yet the memory of her asking Yani over and over again to write her final paper for her stuck with him. She hadn't done enough work to receive an A in any of her classes, let alone even pass them.

"Someone gave her a coercion spell," Aaron stated firmly. "So she can tell someone to do something for her and they have to obey."

"It didn't work on me, though," Yani said thoughtfully. "So it must be something visual." Yani's memory dredged up a flash of all the times Rachel had worn a low-cut shirt so he had an almost uninterrupted view of her boobs. What if the spell was somehow in there? It would explain some of her extreme behavior.

"She probably set the ifrit after you to figure out why you weren't being coerced like everyone else," Aaron sighed.

"Which means she's connected to our summoner," Brandon added. He had met Rachel at least once that Yani knew of, but he had been lucky enough to not be her target. "We should probably talk to her about it."

Bishop was silent through their discussion, just standing next to them as he listened and watched carefully. He had a strange sort of half smile on his face. It didn't make Yani nervous, per se, but he did wonder what Bishop was thinking about the four of them. That was a problem for another day, though. Finding the ifrit and the sorcerer was more important than digging through Bishop's brain.

"Rachel has fixated on Yani this semester," Brandon was continuing when Yani refocused on the conversation. "He should be the one to approach her about what's been going on. When do you have class with her again?" he asked Yani.

Yani grimaced, but he understood their logic. It would raise less suspicion if he was the one, although there was no telling what the ifrit had told her. "Today is Friday," Yani thought aloud, assuming he had slept through only one night. He was missing current events journalism he and Mary were both taking to fulfill their creative arts elective requirement, but he would text Mary later to tell her he was sick and she would give him a copy of her notes. "I've never run into Rachel on Fridays, and I don't think she has a dorm room because I've never seen her on the weekends. The human rights class we're both taking is at 10:40 on Monday morning. After that might be best."

"So we lure her out," Luke said thoughtfully.

"And pounce," Brandon agreed. His smile was wide and showed a few more pointed teeth than a human mouth should have.

"She has an apartment in Boston, just a few blocks from the school," Bishop added. "It would be good if you had the chance to search inside."

"An apartment in the heart of Boston? What did she do, seduce a millionaire?" Aaron grumbled incredulously under his breath. He continued in a louder voice. "If Yani can get into her place and leave the door unlocked, we can sneak in and look around."

"Getting into her place isn't the problem," Yani groaned. "It's what she'll try to do to me once she's got me there. I tried explaining that I was gay to her, but she won't take no for an answer!"

Aaron's immediate scowl at Yani's words was the best thing Yani had seen that day. There was a touch of possessive jealousy there that made Yani's blood heat. He wished they were alone so they could kiss like they had the previous day. Surely they could find a moment for a little private intimacy, even with Yani being stuck in bed.

"She can't seduce you," Luke disagreed with a laugh, thankfully interrupting Yani's train of thought before he had to dive for the blanket to hide the reaction his boxers were too thin to conceal. "We're already sure of that."

Yani forced his gaze away from Aaron to look at Luke. Speaking of seducing... "If I have eyes-that-see, then how come your magic affected me?"

Luke's smile widened, and Aaron grunted at the reminder that Yani had slept with Luke. "Because it wasn't magic," Luke explained. "I am an incubus. Simple as that."

Which explained nothing to Yani.

Aaron sighed and shook his head. "It's what he is. He didn't have to change anything about himself or add to his allure with a spell or potion. There's no illusion involved at all, just Luke being himself."

Yani reached out to grip Aaron's hand in his. The angle was awkward, but he needed to touch his boyfriend to reassure both himself and Aaron that their current relationship was more important than Yani's past with Luke. Aaron squeezed Yani's hand gratefully and shifted his body on the bed so the angle wasn't as bad.

"I'll let you boys put your heads together to plan," Bishop said. "Come find me if you need any advice." He nodded politely to them before turning and leaving the room. Yani couldn't help feeling suspicious of Bishop's motives again. But there were more important things to worry about at the moment. Bishop was a good man and a good werewolf. He wouldn't do anything to hurt his grandson or Brandon's friends. Bishop would no doubt explain himself eventually, so Yani pushed his worries away in order to focus solely on the problem at hand.

There was an ifrit on the loose, and Rachel could be the key to stopping it before something terrible happened.

The dining hall burned down late Thursday night, Mary's text read.

Yani stared at it incredulously, swallowing hard because he had a good idea of why. He and Brandon had escaped the ifrit by getting pulled into the dream plane on Thursday afternoon. The ifrit had retaliated harshly, but it was also probably sending a warning.

Luckily no one was hurt, but they canceled classes on Friday while the police were investigating. You didn't miss anything.

The second text message appeared while Yani was still staring at his phone. She sent a third almost immediately afterward.

Check your email. The school sent out an official message about it. We should have class on Monday, though, so feel better soon!

Yani ignored the half-dozen emoticons after her last text, sent back a quick *Thanks, see you Monday*, and turned his phone off.

They had to stop the ifrit before it could do something worse. Yani had a feeling that Rachel's fixation wouldn't stop with just sending the djinni to interrogate him or allowing it to burn down one building. She could potentially do anything: from burning down the dorm he was supposed to be sleeping in at night—killing dozens of innocent students in the process—to seducing someone in the registrar's office so she could get his home address to go after his family. No one knew to what depth she was willing to allow herself to fall to, although consorting with an evil djinni was pretty damned low in Yani's opinion.

His resolve to do everything he could to stop her hadn't wavered in the least before he heard Mary's news, but it was reaffirmed now. Previously, Yani had felt a little hesitant about allowing Rachel to think he was interested to the point of following her home, and the idea of purposefully leaving her door unlocked so his friends could sneak in to back him up had been fighting with his conscience. That reservation was gone now.

The plan was as firm as they could get it given the few facts they actually knew: Rachel had somehow gone from a girl of little, albeit comfortable, means to the exact opposite. She had seduced her way through school, most likely via an illusion spell hidden in the chest implants Bishop had found a surgical record for, and she was able to send the ifrit djinni, a powerful creature in its own right, on the arbitrary task of finding out why that spell failed in Yani's case.

All Yani had to do was get inside her apartment, which, according to Bishop, had been warded to keep out intruders. Even if he couldn't leave the front door unlocked, thereby creating a hole in the wards that Aaron could break through, once Yani was inside, Luke could pinpoint Yani's location in the dream plane and enter the apartment that way. He could open the door for everyone else while Yani kept Rachel occupied. It was the occupying part that had Yani really nervous, because he knew he couldn't fake sexual attraction to her.

The hours passed slowly as nerves kept Yani awake at night and restless during the day. He didn't leave his bed much, trying to give his legs as much of a chance to heal as he could. Gem'ma had come by twice more, once Friday night and again Saturday morning, to check on him. Yani was feeling healed by Sunday night as the sun set outside his windows and the people he shared the room with started to get ready for sleep. Aaron was in the bunk next to Yani. Brandon and Luke were sleeping at the werewolf house next door.

Aaron's gaze caught Yani's as he slid under the covers. They hadn't been able to speak much the entire weekend, since Yani was recovering and Aaron was running around getting everything ready for Monday, but his eyes said enough. There was heat there, and Yani was just happy for the instant zap of connection between them. When this was all over—the ifrit gone and the summoner brought to justice for his or her crimes—they needed to get together and finally figure out their relationship. One kiss and holding hands was nice, but Yani wanted more, and he had little doubt Aaron felt the same.

It wasn't just about sex either. Yani wouldn't say no to a nice roll in the sheets with Aaron, of course. Aaron had a beautiful body, nicely muscled, and his face featured in quite a few of Yani's daydreams during an extended shower or three. There was also the start of an emotional connection in a relationship they really didn't have a chance to explore yet. They spoke about their families and their favorite things, superficial topics for the most part, but never had any opportunity to go into dreams or wishes. Yani wanted to know all of the things that made Aaron who he was as a person and to give Aaron the same knowledge about Yani. None of that would happen overnight; it required trust and love as well as spending happy and sad times together. Once the drama was finally finished, Yani was going to make forging that connection a priority.

Yani smiled softly at Aaron and was gratified when Aaron smiled in return. One of the other residents grumbled in his sleep, and Yani heard the shifting of blankets across the room for a few seconds before the overhead light abruptly went out and Aaron's face was hidden in the darkness.

Sleep came slowly, but Yani knew there wouldn't be any dreams or nightmares waiting for him that night. No, it was the next morning where those fears would come to the fore instead.

Yakov and Martin sat together on a small couch in one of the sitting rooms in the coalition building. Upstairs, Yani was no doubt asleep, but the night had barely begun for a vampire. Bishop joined them a few moments later. He was carrying a tray with three cups on it. Two were filled with blood that had been generously donated by someone living in the mansion, while the third contained simple tea. The scent of dog still filtered over the other scents, but Bishop could not help what he was any more than Martin could.

"We are not needed here any longer, are we?" Martin asked softly after they all had a moment to sip their drinks. The blood was still warm, almost fresh from the vein, and delicious.

"Children have to grow up sometime," Bishop replied in an equally soft voice. He didn't sound particularly happy about that fact, but he was resolute anyway.

Yakov slowly lowered his cup back to the saucer lying carefully on his bent knee. "Yani is not really a child any longer. I had already been married and widowed with an infant by his age."

"Times have changed," Bishop interrupted gently. "And, from what I understand, your childhood was particularly tumultuous. But if we don't push the child into the water, how will he ever learn to swim? I believe that Yani, Aaron, Brandon, and Luke can accomplish the task set before them." While his voice sounded certain, his face was pale and lined. The stress of the situation was blatantly forcing Bishop's age to show. Brandon was his grandson, Martin knew, and Bishop had a certain fondness for the other boys. Whether Bishop was actually certain or just showing bravado didn't matter. He wasn't going to coddle them through their fight.

"What are you planning?" Yakov asked, his eyes sharp as he studied Bishop. Martin knew Yakov had missed nothing of what Martin had seen.

Bishop sighed and had to put his teacup down before his shaking hands spilled any of the hot liquid. "If they are able to stop the ifrit and discover who the culprit is, they could be of great use to the Northeastern Coalition. We need someone young enough, while still powerful enough, to handle situations that, for various political reasons, I and my many associates cannot."

"And if they don't discover a solution?" Yakov asked. His hands shifted restlessly, so Martin gently took them in his and held on tightly to offer what little comfort he could.

"They'll most likely be dead," Bishop said frankly. His hands were clasped between his knees so the shaking no longer showed, but the sweet perfume of agitated dog began to take over from the scent of blood and tea. "But even your presence in their upcoming fight couldn't ensure their lives."

"Perhaps not," Martin agreed, although it pained him to admit it. "However, I think we will continue to enjoy your hospitality for a few more days, just in case. Should the missing master vampire be located, our help calming him might prove invaluable."

"Stay as long as you like," Bishop agreed readily.

They finished their drinks in silence. Once the cups were empty, Bishop gathered the dirty dishes back onto his tray and left. Martin continued to hold Yakov's hands tightly in his own, offering what little comfort he could to his beloved.

Five:Fire

Class felt like it might never end. Yani glanced at the slowly ticking clock hanging over the classroom door with trepidation. He didn't want class to end because then he would have to approach Rachel. At the same time, the longer class went on, the more worried over the imminent confrontation he grew.

The clock ticked, and eventually Yani's next glance at it showed that class was ending. The professor reminded them that their papers were due soon, as if Yani had the presence of mind to worry about that at the moment, before sending them on their way.

Yani hoped his knees weren't visibly shaking as he gathered his things together and stood up from his desk. Rachel was checking her makeup in a compact mirror and hadn't moved, so Yani waited for his classmates and professor to leave before he approached her.

"I'm sorry about earlier," Yani began, glad when his voice sounded normal. "I didn't mean to hurt your feelings.

Your friend explained how mean I was being. I didn't realize, honest!"

Rachel looked up from her mirror and smiled widely. There was a hint of smug triumph there that Yani would have missed if he wasn't looking for it.

"Oh, Yani," she breathed, her voice low and sultry, "I knew you would come around." Her lower lip jutted out in what was probably supposed to be a sexy pout. Yani tried to look stunned by her beauty instead of disgusted by her selfishness.

"I want to help you with your paper, Chava. To make up for being so awful to you." His earnestness seemed to be working. Rachel was shallow and not too bright—Yani had known that about her for years after watching her skate by on the backs of the boys she seduced—so it didn't surprise him in the least when she smiled brightly at him as if he hadn't purposefully been snubbing her all semester.

She tucked her compact back into her purse, gathered her notebook—filled with doodles instead of class notes, Yani saw as she flipped the cover closed—and got to her feet. Yani couldn't help wondering why she even came to class at all when she could convince the professor to mark her present because of her attraction spell. It was probably to find her next victim, but maybe she liked the idea of learning so attended her classes and didn't want to bother with the actual work involved so she enticed others to do it for her.

"Lead the way," she said with a coy giggle. "Where is your dorm room?"

"Ah," Yani said with as much awkward hesitation as he could put into that one sound. He had practiced his answer to that question so he could reply without making it sound like he was trying to get into her house for a nefarious reason, even though he was. "My roommate asked me to stay out of our room this afternoon. His girlfriend is in town, and he wants to spend some time with her." Rachel immediately laughed, catching on to his insinuation that Brandon was having lots of sex with a girl at the moment and wouldn't appreciate being interrupted. "We could go to your place instead?" Yani asked.

He was really hoping she took the bait. He didn't want to spend hours at the library while she lowered the front of her shirt for his perusal and giggled haplessly as he researched whatever genocide she wanted her paper written about.

"For your roommate," she agreed with another silly giggle. She handed her bag to Yani to carry and then latched onto his arm with her hands, pulling him close so he could feel every curve of her breasts. They walked out of the classroom and through the building like that, Rachel only letting him go for long enough to hold open a door for her.

"Do I need my T card?" Yani asked as they stepped outside, as if he didn't already know where she lived. Brandon was standing next to a tree in the busy quad, a textbook held open in front of his face. He must be close enough that he could overhear, although Yani's human ears certainly wouldn't have been able to make out their conversation from that distance. Rachel didn't notice him.

"It's a quick walk," Rachel explained.

Brandon snapped his book closed and walked away from them. He had the confirmation they needed that Yani's part of the plan was going well. He would join Luke and Aaron hiding outside Rachel's house.

Boston's streets were always busy, especially so near lunch time, but Rachel lived close enough to the school that it wasn't a big problem. She had chosen the location well; her victims didn't have time to realize they were caught before she had them home and locked in her web.

Rachel lived on the top floor of a modest apartment building. The outside was brick, typical of this part of Boston, and well appointed. It wasn't a place someone with college loans could afford. Aaron had already checked the lock on the lobby door and found it untouched by Rachel's spells, so Yani left it alone. Yani followed Rachel inside and to the elevator, another major extravagance, which took them to the fourth floor.

The top floor of the building was split into two penthouse apartments. Rachel's was on the left, and Yani could almost see a line drawn along the floor against the door. It glowed slightly to his eyes, but Aaron said it had taken a search spell for him to locate and identify it. Rachel unlocked the door, but before she could grip the handle, Yani stepped forward.

"Allow me, beautiful," he murmured huskily, pretending he was speaking to Aaron while out on a date. He pushed the door open and gallantly waved her in, as if he were a perfect gentleman.

Rachel giggled and flounced inside, apparently buying his act that her attraction spell had finally started working on him. Yani followed, carefully sliding the door closed behind them. He was really hoping Rachel wouldn't notice it wasn't actually latched.

"Where do you want to do this?" Yani asked, looking around. They hadn't gotten a chance to scope out her apartment before, but it appeared to be fairly ordinary. It had a small entry hallway that opened up to a combination living room and eat-in kitchen. According to the building plans, there were also three bedrooms.

"Let's start on the couch," Rachel purred, her eyes going low as she focused on Yani's chest. "We can go into my bedroom if we need more space later."

Yani reached into his bag to take out a notebook and pen. "So, you're writing your essay on which genocide?" he asked.

Rachel's shirt somehow managed to sink even lower. Yani could see her brown areola peeking out of the top of her bra. She was probably trying to increase the force of her attraction spell, and Yani had to fight his instincts to politely look away. "You don't want to do something more fun first?" she murmured seductively.

That was about as far as Yani was willing to go with a woman. He didn't find her sexy or the least bit desirable. Something about her touch had his skin writhing, and her perfume made him want to scrunch up his face in disgust. Keeping up the farce that he had finally been snared by her spell would be next to impossible if clothing started coming off. Besides, Yani definitely couldn't fake the physical reaction Rachel was expecting. Instead, Yani let the act end. His backup should be on their way up the stairs, so it was the perfect time.

"Why did the mage put the spell in your silicone implants?" he asked coldly. "The coercion and seduction spells are a nice idea, but they really aren't that effective on people who think you're pathetic and sad, Rachel."

She hissed at him, actually hissed like a snake or an angry cat, as she backed away. Her shirt slid back into place, to Yani's relief, but then he noticed the wardrobe fix was coupled with fangs growing in her mouth.

"The ifrit was right," she snarled. "I wouldn't be able to eat you the normal way, but there are other ways of eating human flesh that go beyond simple sex." Her teeth were growing pointier as she spoke, and her face elongated slightly.

"What are you?" Yani gasped. He was trying to stay calm until help arrived, but his heart was beating frantically and his hands were starting to tremble in fear. She was scary! Intellectually, Yani knew there were magical creatures he hadn't even heard of. The coalition building had far too many specialty rooms designed for things that weren't human in any shape. Still, the thing Rachel was morphing into was well outside of Yani's limited imagination.

"What does that matter to you, food?" she hissed back. Her spine was arching as if something were shifting around that really shouldn't be. A line of black drool fell between lips that couldn't close around all the teeth jutting there.

She lunged at him and Yani dove, rolling on the ground to get away. No one had even thought that Rachel might be something other than human. Yani didn't have a knife or anything to defend himself with. All he had were eyes-that-see, and those were pretty useless at the moment.

He stumbled back to his feet and squared his body, just as Sensei had beaten into him. When she lunged again, Yani swung. His fist connected with her face with a crack. She reeled back, and Yani whimpered, feeling his knuckles scream in pain. Actually hitting someone was considerably different than hitting a padded target. Yani ran. He cradled his hurt hand to his chest and headed toward one of the bedrooms. Maybe he could barricade himself inside until help arrived. Aaron, Brandon, and Luke had to be close.

Yani managed to get to the bedroom door. He pushed it open, ran inside, and slammed it shut behind him. With a click, the lock slid into place. Seconds later, the handle rattled and then Rachel screeched. The door thudded as she banged on it, trying to force the hinges or the lock to give way.

"She's one of magic's better creations," a voice said from behind Yani. "Don't you think?"

The ifrit wasn't hiding behind any illusions this time. He was fire held vaguely in the shape of a man. His eyes were burning depths and his mouth a cavern into hell itself. That his feet didn't burn the carpet as he slowly walked closer to Yani was a surprise. Yani plastered himself against the still thudding door. There wasn't anywhere to go. Outside the door was the creature that had been Rachel. Inside was the ifrit.

"I had hoped you might provide more entertainment for me with her. Such a shame your eyes-that-see ruined everything. But that will make it much more fun when I pluck them out of your head." The creature laughed, a crackling of flames that made Yani think of screams of someone dying inside a burning building. Yani was shaking as the ifrit came closer and sweating from the heat in the room. Where were Aaron, Luke, and Brandon? Rachel was still banging on the door, so they hadn't even made it inside the apartment yet.

Yani's hand scrabbled behind him, trying to find the doorknob and the lock. He would take his chances running past Rachel to reach the door outside. He had to because he knew that one more second in the ifrit's company spelled his death.

"Ah, don't run now," the ifrit laughed. "There's still so much fun to have!"

Yani let out a little scream of fright as the ifrit reached forward. One finger gently touched Yani's shoulder, and pain bloomed. Fiery, burning pain. The smell of burnt meat immediately filled the air as Yani screamed, shuddering and crying. His knees hit the carpet without his consent as he bent his body to try to protect that one tiny spot on his shoulder that was radiating pain.

The ifrit tsked, shaking his head as if in regret. "If you can't cope with that, then there's barely any fun to be had." He reached out again and Yani crawled away. He couldn't help it. The futility of his action didn't even cross his mind. He had to get away, had to. The ifrit froze midmotion, giving Yani time to start crawling underneath the bed. It was difficult with only one arm cooperating fully.

With a sigh, the iftrit dropped his arm. "Well, that's a shame. The master calls. Come along, then."

One second Yani was sobbing and trying to hide underneath a box spring, and the next darkness covered his eyes as his stomach was left behind in the sudden movement. Light returned, and his stomach caught up at the same time. Yani dropped a few inches onto a hard floor, falling right on his injured shoulder. He screamed, streamers of red and black flickering across his vision, before darkness returned as he fainted.

Everything was perfectly all right in Yani's world. He felt light as a feather and happy as a lark. There couldn't be any feeling better in the world than the bliss Yani was feeling.

It took a few tries for his eyes to open. The effort that took almost wasn't worth it, but he wanted to see what was causing such goodness so he could replicate it. The ceiling above him looked like stone with stalactites hanging high overhead. That was an odd sight to see, but odd was perfectly okay.

Yani's head flopped sideways, again after a lot of effort. He blinked away sudden stars as his cheek hit the stone slab he was lying on. It didn't hurt; nothing hurt, and for a very brief moment Yani wondered why.

The cavern was large and lit by huge spotlights propped along the walls. A few feet from where Yani was lying were two large cages, like the type he had seen on TV that transported bears or tigers for the zoo. In one cage was a sleeping blond wolf curled around Luke, who also appeared to be sleeping. The wolf must be Brandon. In the other cage was Aaron. He was lying on his side facing Yani. Aaron wasn't asleep, but the way his eyes kept flickering told Yani he wasn't exactly awake either.

Something was wrong. That thought stuck in Yani's head, banishing some of his good feelings. What happened? Yani was doing something with his friends, and now they were in a cavern. What were they doing? Yani couldn't remember. He also couldn't feel his toes.

To get his head to move so he could see his body, Yani had to expend even more effort than before. Gravity wasn't on his side this time, but forcing his neck muscles to obey burned off more of the good feelings clouding his mind. Worry began to creep in.

Yani remembered confronting Rachel. Then it went wrong. Rachel wasn't human, and Yani's backup never arrived. Then the ifrit showed up, and a bad situation quickly got worse. After the pain, though, Yani didn't have any idea what happened. He had passed out, but instead of being dead, he was in a cavern.

With his memories finally restored, finding the will to get his head angled correctly so he could see was almost easy. He had to know what was going on because he was the only one awake enough to do something about it.

He was naked, but his body otherwise looked whole. Someone had painted abstract red lines across his torso and down his abdomen and legs.

"I see you're finally awake," a voice Yani didn't recognize said from Yani's left. The voice sounded young, although given the immortality rates of some of the people Yani had met recently, youth could be an illusion. Yani also couldn't tell what gender the person speaking was. The owner of the voice stepped into view a few seconds later. He or she was covered head to toe in a cloak stolen straight out of the latest fantasy movie. It was wide and billowing to obscure all shape, and a deep hood hid their face. Yani couldn't see any distinguishing features. "I do apologize for not being here when you woke, but I was gathering fresh paint."

The person stepped aside, and out of the corner of Yani's eye he could see what looked like a gigantic metal tripod erected next to the slab he was lying on. A body was hanging upside down from the center of the tripod. Its feet were trussed together by rope tied around the spot where all three metal poles connected. Rachel's body. Yani recognized her hair and the strangely elongated jaw from her apartment. Her throat had been cut so deeply that Yani could see bone and muscle inside. He probably would have gagged had he been able to feel his stomach. As it was, his vision swam for a few long seconds. Placed underneath Rachel was a deep bucket filled with the blood still slowly dripping from her body.

"You see, once it starts to dry, the paint loses efficacy," the stranger continued blandly, as if they weren't talking about a dead girl's blood. Yani refocused on the cloak, if only to keep his mind off Rachel's gruesome death. The person was holding a cup in one long-fingered hand and a paintbrush in the other. Yani couldn't feel the soft bristles or the wet blood as the person dipped the brush and started adding to the lines already covering Yani's body. He still couldn't feel anything, really, nor could he move anything below his neck.

"Wha—" Yani tried to ask. It came out as more of a gasp than a word, but the stranger seemed to get the message.

"Ah, I apologize again," they murmured before dropping the paintbrush back in the cup and reaching toward Yani's neck. After a brief moment, they pulled away again and Yani could feel sensation returning from his collarbone up. "When I woke you the first time, my pain blockers weren't strong enough. I only enjoy tortured screaming when I'm doing the torturing, so I shut off your vocal cords. Try speaking now." The person resumed painting.

"What?" Yani tried. His voice came out clear as if nothing had been blocking it a moment ago. "What are you doing to me? Who are you?"

"Ah, a chatty one. I do so love chatty ones. They talk and they talk until I rip out their tongues. But since you won't be alive for much longer, I suppose I can let it go this time. I'll even answer your questions, if only to allay my boredom from this tedious task. I am writing a spell on your pathetically human body to enhance your innate sight. It's worthless to steal your powers when they're at such a pitiful level. Once my spell is complete, I'll kill you and take your enhanced powers for myself. Eyes-that-see can be quite useful if you know what to do with them. After you're dead, I'll take the power between a mated couple." They gestured in the direction of the cages. "They're so rare, you understand, that I will have to savor their deaths as I make the power that created their bond my own. And then, for my last trick, I believe I will enslave the mage, as I did his idiotic father. So, that answers your first question.

"As to who I am. You may call me Cain. The rest is irrelevant." Cain fell silent as he continued to paint. Yani didn't know how much time passed as dots and swirls were added to the abstract red lines covering his body. Cain left once to refill his cup but returned to work quickly.

"Why can't I move?" Yani asked when the silence grew too ominous. Even if he couldn't feel it, having a dead girl's blood painted on his body was awful. He could imagine how much his skin would be crawling if he could actually feel each line of the paintbrush.

Cain laughed, his voice cold, cruel, and full of arrogance. "Idiot human. Why do you think you can't move? I only erased the rune blocking your speech; the rest are still active." There was nothing but derision in Cain's voice. He swiped the brush a few more times across Yani's body and then stepped away to admire his work. "I'll leave you to marinate for a while. I'll be back once the spell settles in." Cain set the cup aside and strode away.

Yani waited with bated breath, listening hard to hear Cain's footsteps. They receded quickly and then vanished. It was possible he had taken a seat somewhere nearby, but after a few very tense moments when Yani heard nothing except the drip of water from the stalactites and the blood from Rachel's throat, Yani thought Cain might have left entirely.

"Aaron?" Yani hissed. "Luke? Brandon?" They didn't, or more likely couldn't, hear him. Yani hadn't expected them to, but he had hoped they might. Cain was arrogant—Yani could hear that in every word he spoke—but that arrogance meant Cain hadn't realized he had given Yani an escape route. It was probably the only time in his life that Yani was upset that he wasn't overweight. A double chin would make it much easier to bend low enough to rub off the marks circling his neck.

Yani couldn't actually see the marks, and he hadn't felt Cain's finger when he rubbed off one of the runes. He started with the left side of his neck, rubbing his chin as best he could. When nothing happened, Yani slowly moved toward the center of his neck.

Feeling returned to his toes first. Yani couldn't help pausing to give them a wiggle before renewing his ministrations at an even faster pace. The marks were in the center of his neck directly over his Adam's apple. It was the hardest spot to reach, but with every swipe of his chin more movement returned. Soon enough, Yani knew he would be able to lift his arm and use his hand to wipe the remaining runes away entirely.

Yani rubbed his chin further to the right, hoping to get the rest of the rune holding him immobile. Pain hit. Searing, burning pain emanating from his shoulder lit up his body. He could move just fine, Yani found as he cried out involuntarily and curled helplessly around his burnt shoulder. He had forgotten about what the ifrit had done, but there was no forgetting now.

Not screaming was impossible. Yani tried to keep himself quiet though so Cain wouldn't hear him and come to investigate, although Cain was just as likely to let him lie in utter agony as come shut him up. Yani stuffed the hand on his bad arm into his mouth, letting his fingers muffle the sounds he couldn't suppress. Staying in one spot, even if not moving helped with the pain, meant almost certain death. Yani had to roll over.

He let out the loudest scream yet as he rolled and fell off the stone slab. He managed to hit the floor on his good side, but the jolt still rattled his hurt arm. On two legs and one arm, his bad hand still clenched painfully between his now-bloody teeth, he crawled toward the cages.

Brandon and Luke were closer. Yani could barely see through his tears. Sparkles kept flashing across his vision, but Yani refused to black out. He had to get help. He reached between the bars with his good hand and shook Luke's shoulder. Luke's head rolled bonelessly against Brandon's side, but neither opened their eyes. They didn't even twitch when Yani pulled Brandon's tail.

With no other options, Yani struggled around their cage and headed toward Aaron. Yani's hand was dripping blood from where he had bitten through the skin while suppressing his screams. He could feel the blood under his knees as he crawled, but at the same time he couldn't feel the blood that had been painted on. It was an odd sensation.

Aaron's cage was set against a wall. He was probably kept separate because Cain wasn't going to kill him, just enslave him. It took almost everything Yani had to cross the distance. His body was shaking, and he was wheezing. The pain was blinding. Mind shattering. It was a thousand times worse than what Yani's legs had felt like after walking through the dream plane. He collapsed against the side of the cage when he finally reached it.

"Aaron," Yani wheezed, his voice barely better than a whisper as it hitched with pain and tears. His good hand was shaking as he reached through the bars. Aaron was still somewhere between asleep and awake. When Yani's hand slapped ineffectually against Aaron's shoulder, Aaron jumped. His head cracked against the top bar, and he swore as he grabbed the sore spot. Yani felt his body slumping harder against the cage. He didn't have anything left. All he wanted to do was find a way to get the pain to stop. If that was through passing out, then so be it.

"Yani!" Aaron gasped. He reached through the bars, but paused as if he couldn't decide where it was safe to touch. Yani couldn't think enough to find the words to explain. It was taking everything he had to keep his eyes open and his screaming muffled.

Aaron's finger eventually traced something along Yani's throat. As if the sun were breaking through heavy clouds, the pain faded away. It wasn't gone—Aaron's renewal of Cain's spell wasn't nearly as strong—but the difference. God, the difference. Yani's whimpers switched from agony to relief, and his slump lost the rigidity of a body kept stiff so every movement didn't set off more torture. His brain had stopped thinking about anything except getting help, but with Aaron's hand in his, Yani allowed himself to hope for more.

"God, what did they do to you?" Aaron whispered, his eyes taking in the bloody paint.

"My shoulder," Yani replied. He was surprised he had the strength to speak clearly. "But later. We need to get everyone out before Cain returns."

Aaron didn't ask questions. He nodded once before turning his attention to his cage. Aaron's hand didn't let go of Yani's though. After a bit of mumbling, the cage shook and collapsed, nearly sending Yani sprawling painfully onto the ground. Aaron caught him and held him still while Yani wheezed through a renewed flare of pain. Once it faded enough that Yani could see straight, he nodded shakily for Aaron to help him to his feet.

Yani's legs weren't steady enough to support his own weight, but with Aaron's arm holding him up, Yani was able to walk the distance back to Luke and Brandon's cage. Aaron studied their still forms for a brief moment.

"It's just a sleeping spell," he sighed in relief. "Give me a second." Yani clung to Aaron with his good arm while Aaron mumbled and waved with both of his. The cage fell away first with a clang that made Yani wince and look around to see if there was any indication of Cain returning to investigate the noise. Luke's eyes blinked open a moment later, and he swore colorfully as he took in his surroundings.

"I was caught in a dream? Me?" He sounded totally incredulous and offended, but Yani suspected he was hiding fear beneath his more visible emotions. Luke still had an arm wrapped tightly around Brandon, who was snuffling through his nose as awareness slowly began to return. That Cain had somehow managed to trap an incubus inside the realm of dreams just proved to Yani how strong of a monster Cain was. They needed to escape now, before it was too late.

Brandon pushed to his feet and shook his body from head to tail. Luke stood with him, but kept one fist bunched in the fur on Brandon's back just as Yani was holding tightly to Aaron.

"How do we get out of here?" Yani asked sharply. He was running on the last of his energy reserves, and the muted pain sapped a little more as each long minute slipped past. Shaking legs wobbling his body to safety was better than forcing his friends to cart his unconscious body around, but the latter was becoming a real possibility if they didn't hurry.

"I can't jump to the dream plane," Luke said as they all looked around the cavern for a likely escape route. "Sorry, but we can't get away my way."

"We'll just have to walk," Aaron decided resolutely. He wrapped an arm around Yani's waist, taking most of Yani's weight and steadying him. "Let's go."

There was a recessed archway on the nearest wall. Aaron chose that as a likely exit point, although it was probably just a hopeful guess, and started walking. His arm around Yani's back was strong and warm. It was also the only thing holding Yani in a vertical position. He was so tired he was practically seeing double. The archway they were headed toward had a twin only a few feet to the left, but Yani didn't think anyone else could see it. It was hard enough keeping his feet moving without also having to blink repeatedly to clear his vision. Besides, his arm hurt a damned lot.

"I think that's far enough," the ifrit said as he stepped out from behind a stalagmite and directly into their path. "As much as I enjoy knowing how badly I'm going to crush your growing hope, if I let you go any farther, my master will crush me instead. But that's okay," he added with a wide, fire-filled grin. "I don't mind crushing your hope of freedom. I'll probably dream about your expressions for the next hundred years. Entertainment is always an important commodity, you know."

The pain in Yani's shoulder doubled as the ifrit sauntered closer. His knees buckled involuntarily as he groaned and whimpered. Aaron wasn't able to hold all of Yani's weight with one arm, but he helped Yani gently sit on the ground before stepping in front of him protectively.

Magnified

"Be gone, foul creature," Aaron snarled as he waved his hands at the ifrit. Yani's pain-addled vision made it look like a thin wave of multicolored sparkles was flying from Aaron's hands directly at the ifrit, who waved it aside with what appeared to be a burst of flame. No one else jumped at the sight, so Yani knew it was just his exhausted brain filling in the blanks.

The ifrit itself looked odd. It had its usual human-shaped form subsumed by fire, but underneath that layer Yani saw what appeared to be blackness. It was an absence of light and fire that looked completely out of place. There were marks circling that blank space, much like the marks covering Yani's body that were still unblemished despite his crawling around on the floor. The swirls and dots were spinning slowly, as if only by perpetually moving could it keep the demon contained.

There was no way Yani's confused mind could have created that. He was far too injured for his imagination to have been able to come up with something so specific. Instead, it must be his eyes-that-see showing him the truth of the ifrit. The spell written in blood on his body was supposed to enhance his sight, Yani remembered Cain telling him. Perhaps it was taking effect, because Yani hadn't been able to see the runes inside the ifrit before.

Brandon emitted a low growl as he circled the ifrit. Luke was moving in the other direction, a long knife in one hand. Cain had apparently not seen the need to divest anyone of their weapons since the spells were supposed to hold them in place, but Yani knew to use their claws and the knife, Brandon or Luke would have to get too close to the ifrit. They would die in an instant, burned to a crisp.

Aaron was firing more sparkles at the ifrit, but that was proving to be just as inefficient as Luke's knife. The ifrit laughed harder after every desperate attempt.

"Silly, silly humans. Don't give up your pathetic attempts so soon! I'm just starting to have fun!" The ifrit blocked another of Aaron's spells and shot a spout of flame at Brandon, who yelped and dove to the side to avoid getting his fur lit on fire.

"There's a spell around him," Yani hissed at Aaron while Brandon kept the ifrit distracted. The acrid stench of burnt fur filled the cavern as the ifrit sent volley after volley of fire at Brandon, who dodged and jumped as best he could to stay alive. Luke threw a smaller knife at the ifrit to help Brandon, but while the blade hit the creature directly where an eye socket should have been, it didn't have any effect on a creature of fire. The melted knife dripped to the ground as it slowly disintegrated in the flames.

Aaron glanced down at Yani briefly before refocusing his attention on the ifrit. He threw another larger spell the ifrit batted away impatiently. "What does it look like?" he hissed back.

"Like the spell written on me," Yani replied immediately, looking down at Rachel's blood that still wasn't smudged despite all of his stumbling around.

Aaron nodded and narrowed his eyes at the ifrit as if he could force his eyes to see what Yani could. For all Yani knew, Aaron's magic could do that. If they all survived this, Yani was going to start studying. What could mages do? Where did ifrits come from? Perhaps if he had the answers to all these questions, he wouldn't be the one pathetically sitting on the ground while his friends fought for their lives.

"There's a black core underneath the fire," Yani tried to explain. "The spell is circling that."

Brandon's yelp this time was of real pain, and the smell of burning fur intensified. Yani was sweating from the heat of the room. Luke wasn't sweating, but his eyes looked frantic as he tried to find a way to save Brandon from the ifrit's attention.

Aaron threw another spell, one that Yani thought he had already tried. The ifrit turned away from Brandon for the few seconds it took to swat the spell away.

"Got it," Aaron murmured. "It's a power spell. I think it's what's holding the ifrit's power in this plane and under the control of his master. I think I can send it back home, but I need time to set the spell first."

Yani nodded. "I'll help distract it. Don't take too long." He staggered to his feet, his shaking knees just barely able to hold his weight after his brief rest. Brandon's whimpering cries and Luke's panic hardened Yani's resolve as he stepped toward the ifrit and away from Aaron. "There's nothing inside you," Yani told the ifrit. "Just emptiness."

The ifrit laughed again. "I'm a demon, you pathetic human. Of course there's nothing inside." He turned to look closer at Yani. "You're the one with eyes-that-see. I promised that I would pluck out your eyes, didn't I?" It laughed some more. "Let's have some fun!"

Fire bloomed between them, growing in size like a flower unfurling its petals. The ifrit was still laughing as the flame grew and shaped itself into a hand.

"Let's do this slowly. One eyeball at a time!" The hand drifted closer, dripping fire onto the stone floor as it moved through the air in Yani's direction. Running would be useless in Yani's condition, not that he thought distance would help him at all. That didn't stop his feet from shuffling involuntarily backward a few staggering steps. "Pluck one out, see how it tastes. Get it? *See* how it tastes?" The laughter got louder as the ifrit giggled at its own horrible pun.

The ifrit let the hand slowly approach Yani. It probably thought Yani's frozen expression of panic and anticipated pain was fun. Brandon and Luke both tried to distract the ifrit, but he ignored them as he made the pointer finger and the thumb on his fiery hand pinch together as if he were practicing the movement needed to pluck out Yani's eyes. It was ignoring Aaron too, which was what Yani was hoping for. He stumbled back another few steps, moving farther away from the slowly approaching hand and from Aaron.

The hand kept moving. The air was already hot from the fire the ifrit had been using, but Yani could feel it getting even warmer as the hand got close enough to hover in front of his face. He felt like he had bent over an open oven. The whoosh of hot air against his face was uncomfortable and made him sweat, but it wasn't scary. What was scary was the hand. It froze, palm open, a few inches from Yani's face.

It was red and yellow and vibrant blue. Little flickering flames the size of candles mixed with the larger flame of a bonfire. All of it was held together by what appeared to be a thin membrane of more fire. Yani wasn't breathing as he stared into the hand of his probable death. There wasn't air to actually breathe, as the heat from the fire sucked all the oxygen away.

"Look closely, eyes-that-see," the ifrit whispered dramatically. "The last thing you'll see in this life is me, and I want you to remember me forever."

Yani's knees were locked in place. That was probably the only reason he was still standing instead of lying helplessly on the floor. He could honestly say he would never, ever forget what that hand looked like as it hovered impatiently over him.

"In the name of the Malachim, I call you, ifrit djinni!" Aaron's voice was strong, and it echoed slightly in the cavernous space. There was power in his voice, and the flickering flames in the hand froze in place as he continued to call on the angels for aid in his spell. "In the name of the Seraphim, I seal you, ifrit djinni! And in the name of the Ophanim, I banish you, ifrit djinni! Thrice blessed, thrice named, by the power of the Chayot Hakodesh, your time on earth has come to an end!"

Magnified

The hand vanished abruptly with a cracking sound that left behind acrid smoke. Yani's knees collapsed, and his butt hit the ground as he gasped for breath. Through the afterimages caused by the bright light of the fire, Yani could see Aaron.

Aaron had bright wings of light on his back. They were feathered and glowing, the epitome of angel's wings. A spell very similar to the one Yani had seen around the ifrit was circling Aaron. He had called on the angels for his spell, and they had answered.

The wings flapped once. The cavern's air wasn't disturbed by the movement, but the circling spell left Aaron and arrowed directly toward the ifrit. The creature of fire was banked, frozen in place like a still-life portrait. It couldn't put up any defense as the spell hit it directly in the chest. Yani could see the original spell around the blackened core fizzle and fade away. The new spell replaced it, and as the spell settled in, the ifrit began to fade.

Yani thought he could hear screaming, but it wasn't sound in the same way his extra sight wasn't really seeing. And then the ifrit was gone.

The bright wings took a few more moments to fade away, but when they did, Aaron collapsed. His body hit the ground bonelessly. Pain bloomed in Yani's shoulder until he couldn't help crying out. He collapsed on the ground, too, unable to struggle closer to Aaron to see if he was okay.

"Shit," Luke swore. "Brandon, we need your arms more than we need claws." He hurried over to Aaron's side and swore again. "He slashed his wrist to get enough blood for that spell!"

Brandon whined as his body rippled. His fur split and bones cracked as they rearranged their shape to accommodate a human form. The canine whine changed into a human groan as a naked Brandon emerged where the wolf had once stood.

"Grab Yani. We need to get to help fast." Luke had pulled his shirt off and was pressing it to Aaron's wrist as he stood with Aaron's body in his arms.

Brandon was as gentle as he possibly could be given the speed Luke was urging him to. Yani still let out a whimpering scream as his shoulder was accidentally jostled as Brandon lifted him off the ground too. Luke led the way to the wide archway in the cavern wall. Aaron had been right in guessing that it was a doorway, but there was something wrong with it. Luke reached out instinctively via some sixth sense to touch the doorway first instead of just walking through. Yani wasn't surprised when Luke's fingers met solid wall. The real door was to the left.

"Over there," Yani hissed through his teeth. His good arm pointed to the real door, the one that had made it look like he had double vision only ten minutes prior. Luke followed Yani's pointing and reached out toward what appeared to be solid wall to the naked eye. His hand passed through easily. Luke immediately stepped forward, Brandon tight on his heels. The archway was dark for a moment—Yani couldn't see anything, even with his enhanced sight—and then they rushed out into bright sunlight.

They were standing in Rachel's living room. The space was a mess, couches tossed and gouges from Rachel's claws along the walls and floors, but it was recognizable as the place Yani had left not too long ago. A cell phone was plugged into a charger on the wall. Luke grabbed it and dialed one-handed.

"We need healers," he snapped into the other end. He added the address quickly, no doubt recognizing the scenery outside the window, then slammed the phone down on the table and spun away. "You and Yani need clothes," he continued to Brandon, his frantic pace unabated. "I'm going to see if there are bandages in the bathroom."

Magnified

Yani wanted to say that they couldn't stay in Rachel's apartment. Cain could be just behind them. They needed to keep running, not stay in one place and wait for reinforcements. Before he could say any of that aloud, Brandon bent over to pick something up off the floor and accidentally bumped Yani's shoulder into the corner of one of the tossed couches. His scream was cut off only when darkness claimed his vision and he knew no more.

Cain watched from his perch high in the air on one of the stalactites as his creature of fire finally stepped into view, stopping the futile escape party in their tracks. He had summoned the beast to handle these sort of issues. There was no reason for Cain to dirty his hands with a bunch of humans so far beneath him. They were good enough to take power from, but worthless if left alive.

Watching the wolf get burned and the incubus cry was worthy of popcorn. Cain couldn't help lamenting that he didn't have the time to make some, but he didn't want to miss any of the fun.

It was gratifying to see that his spell on the human with eyes-that-see was effective. It was the first time he had tried such a thing, and while he'd known he could do it, he was pleased to see the positive results firsthand.

The pitiful creatures continued to fight, and his ifrit became creative. Cain would have to remember the hand of fire for plucking out eyes in the future. That move was practically inspired; he hadn't thought his ifrit capable of such advanced planning.

And then Cain smelled blood and magic. The entire cavern was soaked in it already, but this blood was full of good intentions. It soured his stomach with its pleasantness. Cain watched the mage work with a frown. He wasn't just a mage, Cain quickly realized, but also a Kabbalist. That threw a bit of a wrench in things. Cain wasn't surprised to see his demon banished once the mage's true power was revealed.

From his perch high above, Cain smirked to himself. Enslaving that mage was useless. He couldn't access that type of power that way. He could absorb it, just as he was going to absorb the power of the eyes-that-see. But maybe later. The ifrit had been correct that the best way to destroy someone was to allow them a chance at the hope of freedom. He would let those four pathetic creatures leave. They could live and grow stronger for at least a few more months. He would let them believe he forgot them so they would come to believe they might best him the next time they met.

It would bring him such joy to utterly destroy that belief when he killed them. It would make the moment so much sweeter.

Once they were back in the human world, Cain sealed off that doorway. No one would be entering his domain through that portal again.

Cain slipped from his perch and let his body fall the distance to the ground. He had a mess to clean up, and then perhaps he would finally put those vampires he had been keeping aside for a rainy day to good use.

Not knowing where he was when he woke was becoming all too familiar to Yani, and he was quickly growing to hate it. Before becoming involved with the coalition, Yani had never experienced waking and not knowing where he was or how he got there. Admittedly, barring a few exceptions, he always woke in his bed at home or in his dorm room. At least this time he wasn't lying on a hard stone slab.

The bed beneath him was soft, and the pillow under his head was perfect. He didn't want to move, especially since he remembered how much pain he had been in before he had fainted. He could feel all his toes and fingers, and it didn't hurt to wiggle them, which mean this wasn't a cruel repeat of Cain's spell. Yani also wasn't alone in the bed. Someone was breathing next to him, and the mattress was shifting slightly with that movement.

He had felt good and pain-free back in the cavern, and the first thing he had done once some form of reality returned was turn his head and see a nightmare brought to life. It wasn't hard to engage the muscles to turn his head now, but he tensed in fear as he did it.

Aaron was sleeping peacefully at Yani's side. He looked pale and drawn, but his forehead was smooth so he didn't appear to be in any pain. Yani remembered a vague conversation about blood loss, but Aaron looked like he was doing okay. Yani let out a soft sigh of relief. Aaron wasn't a nightmare, and it didn't seem like any nightmares were forthcoming.

Yani's bad shoulder was completely numb. He couldn't move it at all, but after a quick investigation under the blankets, Yani found thick white bandages wrapped around his arm and chest that were holding his arm completely immobile. Someone had patched him up, which probably meant they had escaped Cain.

He had to turn practically all the way onto his stomach so he could reach out and touch Aaron with his good arm. He needed that physical touch to confirm what his eyes were telling him about Aaron's health. Aaron's hair was soft and his skin smooth beneath Yani's fingertips. He didn't feel hot or clammy, like he would if he had a fever.

Yani's fingers continued to stroke through Aaron's hair, mindlessly taking comfort from the silky feeling and the knowledge that Aaron was okay. His eyes unfocused slightly as he stared blindly straight ahead.

They had survived. Somehow. Yani had honestly been convinced they were about to die. Rachel's attack, the ifrit, Cain, and then the ifrit's return. He shuddered slightly at the memory of growing fangs and fiery hands.

Yani's hand froze in place on Aaron's forehead as he fought the memory back. He was breathing a little quickly from remembered terror, so he focused on his still fingers. Yani's skin was unblemished despite the fact he had punched Rachel in the face with that hand. It had hurt, and he'd thought he had cut himself, but any evidence of it was gone. There were faint lines on the back of his hand, though. They were slightly jagged as they traveled to his wrist and up his arm. Yani's eyes couldn't help following those nearly indistinct lines up his forearm and to his elbow.

The lines were red, Yani realized quickly, and the swirls, corners, and dots were vaguely familiar. Yani's body had been cleaned of the dirt and blood from the fight, but that didn't mean all the blood was removable. He was looking at Cain's enhancement spell still inked into his skin like a horrible tattoo.

He snatched his hand back from Aaron's head and tried rubbing the lines out. His skin burned as he frantically rubbed and rubbed. The faint red lines did begin to fade, but only because his skin turned a darker shade of red that concealed the spell.

"This isn't how I imagined our first morning together in bed," Aaron groaned. Yani jumped in surprise and spun to look at Aaron. He was pressing the heels of his hands into his eyes as he spoke instead of looking around. With a tired groan, he dropped his hands back to the bed and turned to look at Yani. "What are you doing?" he gasped.

"Trying to get Cain's marks off," Yani growled, his fingers still pulling at his skin as if he could force the marks away.

Aaron grimaced and muttered a few words under his breath as he looked at Yani. "I can't see the runes without a spell," he explained. He slowly sat up, his body slightly stiff and shaky, and reached out to take Yani's reddened hands in his own. "They'll keep fading away until the spell is fully absorbed by your body. Even you won't be able to see them once that happens. I promise, Yani."

Aaron's hands were warm in Yani's own. His nails were a little ragged and his fingers chapped from the unseasonably cool autumn weather. One wrist had a thick bandage around it, but otherwise they were just Aaron's hands. No magic, no trickery.

Yani looked up from their clasped hands. Aaron was still looking at Yani, although without any spells this time. His eyes were tired, the bags underneath them dark and prominent, but they were also kind. There was love there. Yani nearly gasped aloud at that realization. Aaron's eyes were so soft and unwavering as he stared at Yani that Yani couldn't help staring back. He hoped his own feelings were also visible for Aaron to see. Even if they weren't, there was no mistaking Yani's intentions as he tilted his head slightly and bent forward to carefully press his lips to Aaron's.

Yani didn't know if he loved Aaron yet—it was far too early in their budding relationship for him to be capable of saying for certain—but everything he knew about Aaron meant Yani's feelings were quickly heading in that direction. Besides, Aaron was hot and funny, and he understood the scary memories Yani had running through his head. That was deeply important to Yani.

Aaron's response was immediate. His hands tightened around Yani's as he pressed forward to meet Yani's lips. The kiss started out chaste, just the press of lips on lips and the shared breath between them. Yani wasn't certain who opened for more first, nor could he complain about it. Their tongues tangled wetly, and Yani groaned as heat immediately traveled south.

Their clothing needed to go. Yani tried to articulate that fact through a moan. His bound arm was useless and Aaron's hands held him still, but he was aching for the touch of cool air and Aaron's warm hands on his body, particularly since he was half-hard. Yani knew Aaron could bring him to the edge with just a few firm strokes. Yani wanted to return the favor. He wanted to feel Aaron's skin over firm abs, to play with the short hairs covering Aaron's thighs, and to reach between and take Aaron's velvety cock in his hand. Just the thought of it made him even harder. His dick was beginning to strain against the cloth of his pajama bottoms.

"I guess this is a bad time to interrupt," Uncle Yakov said from behind Yani.

Yani jumped, accidentally knocking his forehead against Aaron's in surprise, and scrambled to make sure the blanket was covering his hard-on. Uncle Yakov was standing in the doorway to the room. Bishop was standing next to him, and Yani could also see Gem'ma standing there too.

"We were just going to check on our patients," Bishop added, his voice light with what Yani guessed was laughter despite his otherwise stoic face. He was a werewolf and had probably walked in on situations like this one before, but that didn't lessen Yani's embarrassment or make his blood travel north any faster. "I can see you're both feeling much better, but the doctor would like a closer look."

Bishop stepped aside so Gem'ma could stomp into the room. He didn't look particularly pleased to be there, but as before, Gem'ma knew what he was doing and he did it forcefully, yet kindly. He went to Aaron first and began unwinding the thick bandages circling one wrist.

Aaron had sliced open his wrist for that last spell, Yani vaguely remembered. Everything from that last battle was fogged over in his mind from pain and from being on the edge of passing out. Yani remembered beautiful white wings of magical power and Aaron invoking the angels to banish the ifrit, but nothing afterward.

The bandages were still white as they fell onto the bed in a heap. Only the innermost layer had any staining, but that was from some sort of creamy goop that had been rubbed around Aaron's wrist.

"Barely even a scar," Gem'ma remarked smugly as he turned Aaron's wrist from side to side in his hairy grip. "You'll be getting some real training before you try any blood spells again," he added firmly to Aaron, his eyes very serious from where they were visible between all of his facial hair. "I've healers who can show you where to cut that will still draw arterial blood for the spell without gushing everywhere and killing you."

"And I have a mage who specializes in blood spells who has agreed to take you on," Bishop added.

"I won't work with a dark mage," Aaron said firmly. He had let himself be manhandled quietly and had been staring at his unmarked wrist while he was chastised, but when he looked up, Yani could see the relief on his face and the resolve in his eyes.

Bishop sighed. "All blood mages are dark mages, even if you're calling on the angels. The one I've found will respect your limits."

"Fine," Aaron grumbled. He reached for a tissue on the bedside table to wipe the last of the healing goop off his wrist. "What about Yani?"

Gem'ma and Bishop turned their attention to Yani now that Aaron's injury was out of the way. Had they chosen to check on Aaron first because his injury was the more serious one or to get the easy one done first?

It took a while for Gem'ma to unwind the heavy bandages holding Yani's arm immobilized. He had to walk around Yani on the bed as he worked; his height prevented him from a more dignified position, and his pride was no doubt what kept Bishop from offering to help. Yani tried to hold still as the bandages came off, but his anxiety was mounting. There had been something terribly wrong with his shoulder, and the absence of pain didn't mean that Gem'ma's magic had been strong enough to fix it.

Finally, the last circle of bandages slipped off Yani's body to pool in his lap. Like Aaron's, Yani's bandages were unblemished white. They didn't even have goop on them.

"I fixed the broken knuckle and the bitten fingers easily," Gem'ma grunted. He was stalling, Yani thought as real worry began to creep in. What was so wrong with Yani's shoulder that even an experienced healer like Gem'ma didn't want to talk about it? "Your shoulder was a different matter," he continued after a long exhale. "The skin, bone, and muscles were all melted in a quarter-inch wide circle. It went three inches deep into your shoulder. Another half inch and your collarbone, rib cage, and eventually your lungs might have started melting as well. You wouldn't have survived for long with your lungs on fire, so you were lucky, boy."

As he spoke, Gem'ma poked around Yani's shoulder. His fingers prodded in a circle along the joint and then slowly moved outward. Yani remembered the tip of the ifrit's finger barely touching his shoulder. It had caused that much damage with only a fingertip? Yani probably had gotten off lucky, but he didn't feel like it at the moment. He really wanted to know if he would still have that shoulder and the arm attached to it in the morning.

"I couldn't unmelt you. The damage was far too catastrophic to your body, and any human doctor would probably have had no other option but to cut the arm off at the shoulder. I was able to excise the melted bone and muscle and encourage the parts that weren't melted to hell and back to attempt regrowth." His fingers reached the spot the ifrit had touched. That small area was numb. Yani couldn't feel the feathery hairs hanging off of Gem'ma's knuckles or the press of his callused fingers. "It seems I was successful," he continued, his voice lilting upward in surprise.

Yani finally turned to look. He had been staring at the white bandages still lying in his lap, but hope surged at Gem'ma's last words and Yani found the courage to turn his head.

Gem'ma was focused intently on Yani's shoulder, his eyes fixed where his fingers were pressed. Yani had a feeling Gem'ma was looking underneath Yani's skin to the healing underneath, but Yani's eyes could only see what was on the surface. At first he saw fire. It was the size of a Hanukkah candle flame and barely noticeable when he wasn't looking directly at it, yet it was still the worst inferno Yani had ever seen. It was the burst of crackling flame that brought down ancient trees in a forest fire or destroyed buildings with a wild flare of oxygen. It was terrible while still being only the size of Yani's thumbnail.

Yani blinked, wishing he could rub his eyes while still not yet daring to move his body until Gem'ma was finished. The flame vanished. Yani blinked again and the fire flickered back into view. Gem'ma's fingers wandered directly through it without flinching, which was when Yani realized he wasn't seeing a fire that anyone else could see. It was his messed-up eyes that made the flame visible. He blinked one last time, willing his sight away, and was relieved when the fire disappeared again.

The circle Gem'ma had spoken about was visible on Yani's skin. It was shiny and red and slightly sunken against the rest of his skin. The outer edges of the circle still looked blackened.

"You're a damned lucky kid," Gem'ma repeated as he pulled away.

"The whole family is lucky," Uncle Yakov murmured. "Otherwise we would all be ash in the remnants of the Nazis' chimneys. We were never meant to burn, and that's probably why Yani didn't succumb either."

Gem'ma cast Uncle Yakov a side-eyed look that Yani couldn't interpret. What was Yakov implying? Gem'ma didn't seem to know, and Yani didn't either.

"Anyway," Gem'ma continued. "I'm going to wrap your shoulder again to keep you immobile for a few more days while the bone and muscle recover. You should have full use of your shoulder and arm by the end of the week." Yani let out a breath of relief at that, glad that he could forget the worries about amputation that were still on his mind. "You'll always have that scar. There's nothing I can do about it, but you can tell everyone it's a tattoo gone wrong and no one will ask too many questions."

"I can't get buried in a Jewish cemetery with a tattoo!" Yani grumbled automatically, used to his mom's constant guilt trips about keeping his body clean while away in the wild world that was college.

Aaron let out a snort of laughter, and Yani joined him a moment later. It was so absurd to be channeling his mother about such an insignificant topic. No one else was laughing, but they probably didn't get the joke. Yani continued to chortle as Gem'ma wrapped his arm firmly against his body with fresh bandages.

"We should talk about what happened," Bishop said, immediately sobering both Yani and Aaron's laughter. "I need to know everything you saw. You especially, Yani, since I believe you had a chance to speak with the culprit."

Yani swallowed heavily and nodded. Bishop was correct. If the coalition wanted to mount a defense or offense against Cain, they needed to know just what they were up against.

Gem'ma finished with Yani's bandages and climbed off the bed. He nodded politely to Bishop before leaving the room. Yani assumed he would be back to check on Yani's bandages at some point, but that he also didn't want to hear what had caused Yani's terrible injuries. Yani waited until the door was closed behind Gem'ma before he spoke.

"How are Brandon and Luke?" Yani asked first. Finding out how his friends were doing was just as important, and he felt guilty for not thinking of them sooner.

"Brandon's a little crispy, but werewolves heal better than humans," Bishop replied kindly. He pulled a chair up to the side of the bed next to Yani and sat. Uncle Yakov remained standing, but his presence was comforting. "Luke wasn't hurt physically by the confrontation. He informed me quite succinctly that he would be training his dreaming abilities over the next few weeks because he wasn't going to get caught in his own dreams again. I believe there may have been some psychological damage, but he appears to be dealing with it admirably. They, like you and Aaron, were given one of our few single rooms to share while they heal. I won't go into detail about how they are enjoying their healing time together, but given where you both were headed, I think you can safely guess."

Bishop stopped speaking and waited expectantly for Yani to fill the silence. Yani took a deep breath to brace himself for the terrible memories he was about to relive and started to speak.

"The original plan was to corner Rachel and force her to tell us who was helping her," Yani began. His hand crept sideways until he found Aaron's, and then he gripped tightly. "My job was to get inside the protection wards she placed around her apartment and leave a hole for the others to enter through. That part went smoothly. The problems began when I refused to have sex with Rachel, and my backup didn't arrive. Rachel began to shift." Yani paused to think. He had seen Brandon change from a wolf to a human, and he remembered the terrible popping of bones and cartilage as Brandon groaned in pain. Rachel hadn't exhibited any of those symptoms. "Not shift, exactly. It was more like she dropped the illusion hiding her real self."

Bishop hummed. "If it was merely an illusion, I suspect you would have seen through it long ago."

"It was probably a glamour," Aaron interjected. "That's a lot stronger than an illusion, and some of them are inherent to the creature that uses them, like Luke's attraction is to him. You might not have been able to see through that."

Might not have been able to then, Yani wondered as he looked down at the faint red lines still crisscrossing his arms. Would a glamour stop him now?

"Anyway, she grew lots of pointed teeth, and her spine started bending the wrong way," Yani gasped out quickly. The sooner the words were out of his mouth, the sooner he could return to trying to forget everything that had happened. Only time blunted bad memories and that time wouldn't begin until after his story was told. "I hit her to escape and ran. I was going to barricade myself in a bedroom until backup arrived, only the ifrit was waiting for me. He—" Yani choked on spit and shuddered as the memory of the ifrit's merest touch burning through his arm resurfaced with full intensity. "He hurt my arm, and then I blacked out."

"So Rachel and the ifrit were both creatures summoned by the enemy to do the dirty work," Bishop agreed. "Aaron, why don't you fill in the missing portion? Where was Yani's backup?"

Aaron groaned. "Good damned question. We saw Yani and Rachel go into the apartment building. We only waited a minute to let them get upstairs before following. I was behind Luke and Brandon as we walked through the front door, and the next thing I knew was Yani slapping me awake."

"I was in a cavern," Yani jumped in, desperate to get to that point in his own story. "I couldn't move or speak, and a person in a big cloak was painting symbols all over my body. He called himself Cain, when I asked," Yani rushed on, hoping to skip having to explain where the paint had come from.

"When you asked?" Bishop inquired. His voice was lightly curious, a sharp contrast to Yani's rushed and panicked one, but Yani doubted he was missing anything of what Yani was saying or of what Yani also wasn't saying.

"I tried to speak first. When that didn't work, Cain rubbed a symbol off my neck. He told me he had to write a spell on my body to enhance my eyes-that-see so they would be at their most powerful when he killed me and stole them. When he finished writing, he left and I was able to rub off the spell holding me still. I couldn't wake Luke or Brandon where Cain had them locked in a cage nearby, but Aaron was under a different spell. Cain said he wanted to enslave Aaron like he had Aaron's father. Anyway, Aaron woke up and freed everyone. We ran for the exit, but the ifrit showed up again. Aaron banished it," Yani plowed on as his mind tried to supply images of that fiery hand coming closer, "and we escaped. I passed out afterward, but since we made it back here safely, I assume you reached us in time."

"Enslaved my father?" Aaron asked at the same time that Bishop exclaimed, "You were able to banish an ifrit!"

"That's what Cain said," Yani told Aaron while Aaron ducked his head to hide an embarrassed blush.

"It's Kabbalah," Aaron explained to Bishop. "My mother taught me."

Bishop hummed noncommittally to himself, but Yani thought his eyes got a little sharper as he studied Aaron. "Can you tell me if this Cain was male or female?" he asked as his attention returned to Yani. Yani shook his head wordlessly in response. "Cain sounds like an unseelie sidhe. Interesting that he chose to use the name Cain, given the biblical implications. I will have to do some research on this incident. Both of you, rest. Once you're healed, we'll speak again."

The chair squeaked as he pushed away from the bed and stood. Once he was gone, Yani couldn't help letting out a sigh of relief. He never had to relive those memories again. He could pack them away to the back of his brain where the horrors could stay hidden in the dark where they belonged.

"Martin and I are going to be returning home in a few days," Uncle Yakov said softly. "We would honestly be more of a hindrance than a help against Cain, and our affairs back in Poland have gone unanswered for long enough."

Yani looked up at Uncle Yakov in surprise. "Do you really have to go?" he asked, surprised at just how much sadness was in his voice. He hadn't spent nearly enough time with his uncles to get so attached, and yet they were his tangible link between the supernatural world and his mundane human family. Yani wanted the comfort of family around him, especially now that he had nightmares lurking in his brain that were just waiting for an unguarded moment to strike.

"We do. Martin can't be away from his territory for too long without another master vampire trying to move in." He reached into his pocket and pulled out a slip of paper. "Here is our phone number. Call if you have any problems or if you just want to talk."

Yani took the paper and looked down at the international phone number written there. "Thank you," he said softly. He didn't only mean for the number, of course, since Uncle Yakov and Uncle Martin coming to town had saved Yani from so many things.

By the time Yani looked up, Uncle Yakov was gone and the door was swinging open to let Luke and Brandon into the room.

"We heard you were awake, so we came to say hi," Brandon explained. "Also, Yani, I brought your laptop if you wanted to finish your homework since I'm pretty sure it's due in a couple of days."

Finishing his essay on a genocide wasn't exactly high on Yani's list of priorities at the moment, but he reached out with his good arm to take the bag from Brandon. School was continuing without him and so was life. Uncle Yakov was returning to his, and it was about time for Yani to put aside the past few weeks and get his own life back on track. He grinned at Brandon and Luke.

"I'm surprised you're both walking, considering Bishop said you were fucking like bunnies the last time he checked on you both."

"Yani!" Aaron gasped, but he was laughing. They were all laughing. Banged and bruised they might be, but they had survived the fire. Somehow, they had survived.

Mell Eight

The girl was somewhere between the indeterminate age of fourteen and sixteen. Puberty had hit and her breasts and hips were grown, but she looked unfinished. The impression of more growth was mostly centered in her face. She still looked young, too young. And yet, she had been dead more than a hundred years. Surviving for that length of time as an underdeveloped vampire was a feat in itself. She was powerful, but had chosen to pretend to be mundane because she didn't look like she could lead. That was about to change.

Martin was kneeling in front of her so his head was only a little lower than hers while she was standing. "You're the only one who can take over the Boston coven," he repeated again when she hesitated to place her hands in his. With Cain on the loose, it was a fair assumption that the previous master would not be returning in any shape to retake command of his coven, should he return at all. "I can give you enough power to make your position stick."

"Fine," she snapped, and slapped her hands in Martin's.

Martin gathered his power and thrust it at her. She absorbed it immediately, her own powers taking his almost greedily. No doubt it was involuntary on her part, but once she realized what was happening, she immediately tried to grasp more. Martin gently blocked her and then shaped the power she had already absorbed to one specific purpose.

She aged right in front of Martin's eyes. Her cheekbones filled out and she grew three inches in height. She also grew another cup size, which made her shirt really strain in the front. Since Martin's eyes were unfortunately placed directly in front of her chest after she grew upward, he noticed that change. Yakov could admonish him for it later, which would be a pleasant diversion.

Her indeterminate age was somewhere between eighteen and twenty-two by the time her borrowed power ran out.

Magnified

"I understand that you've given me the ability to command this coven, but I will not be beholden to you," she said firmly as Martin let go of her hands and stood.

"I have my own coven back home to worry about," Martin replied just as firmly. "So long as you grant Yakov and I permanent visiting rights to your territory, we will never have an issue."

She hesitated for the briefest moment as if weighing whether she could get away with denying Martin that one boon. In the end, she nodded. No doubt she knew some of the reasons why Martin was going to visit and just how nonnegotiable that caveat was. "Granted," she replied formally. "Just don't give me any reason to regret that decision."

With that last parting shot given, she spun and walked out of the room with her head held high. No doubt she would find new clothing that actually fit before confronting the coven that had started growing unruly without their master. Martin hadn't been willing to leave the area without ensuring some protections for Yani were in place, and having a stable coven was one of them.

Once she was gone, Yakov walked out of a bit of convenient shadow. He stopped at Martin's side and wrapped one arm over Martin's shoulder. "I have a willing donor waiting for you, my love." Martin did need to regain his strength before their journey home after using so much of it, but dear Yakov had already planned for that.

Martin allowed himself to be led away, gratefully leaning against Yakov's side as they walked.

"Ready to return home, beloved?" Martin asked.

Yakov smiled. "Oh, yes," he agreed.

Epilogue

All four of his youngsters were seated and chatting with each other by the time Bishop arrived. Brandon, his grandson, was mostly sitting in the lap of his lover. Luke, the incubus who had somehow snared a werewolf, had both hands buried in various places on Brandon's body that Bishop didn't want to think too deeply about.

Sitting on the couch next to them were Yani and Aaron. Yani was the weak link, yet he was also the reason the group had formed at all. He was Brandon's roommate who had inadvertently introduced his ex-boyfriend Luke to Brandon. He was also Aaron's lover. Without Yani, this group of boys would never have joined together. Bishop sometimes wondered if the Supernatural Coalition would have survived the attack of the ifrit sent by its master, Cain, without Yani's interference.

Aaron was the wildcard in the group. He was devoted to his friends and appeared to be devoted to the coalition's cause of keeping the world calm and safe for all creatures. Aaron was a powerful mage who had studied the obscure art of Kabbalism. Should he turn on the coalition, Bishop didn't know if there was anyone living close enough who could stop him before the coalition was nothing but smoke. It was sobering to think the main reason Aaron would remain their ally was his relationship with Yani.

As a regular human, even with his eyes-that-see, Yani shouldn't be part of anything supernatural. Yet here he was. Here all four of them were. And Bishop had to do something to keep them all together and working with the coalition.

Bishop stepped into the sitting room and let the door softly close behind him. There was a large armchair still unoccupied across from the two couches. Bishop sat there and then paused to gather his thoughts.

"I have a proposition for you," he said when he was ready. "There isn't any such thing as a police force or a jury in the supernatural world. The different species generally police themselves, to be honest, and wouldn't welcome outside interference. However, as the world becomes a smaller place, the different species are being forced to interact more and more often, and interspecies conflicts continue to crop up. At such a time they are either able to resolve the conflict through bloody or peaceful means or they turn to the coalition for unbiased arbitration. We are hoping to encourage the latter option as it tends to result in less violence and, more importantly, fewer chances for the human world to notice that we exist."

He hadn't lost them yet, Bishop was happy to see as he paused to gauge their reactions. Yani was interested in international law, Bishop knew, and he was the one Bishop needed to convince because he would bring the other three with him. This was sort of like international law, with different species from across the world with their own customs and traditions involved.

"The problem arises when two parties journey to the coalition house where they each tell me their side of the story and expect a ruling in their favor. There are never just two sides to any story, and often so many facts are left out that a fair ruling is almost impossible to give. I need a group willing to travel to the locations in question to speak with everyone involved, investigate the issue at hand, and bring their unbiased findings back to the coalition."

"You want to hire us," Aaron stated. He didn't sound resistant to the idea, but Bishop was hoping he could sweeten the pot a little.

"It will allow you all to hone your skills and grow. Should Cain resurface, you will be prepared thanks to this position. It's a full-time, salaried job with the coalition, including health benefits and a retirement savings plan, just like any job. We'll even spin it so it shows up in federal and state taxes," he added, which seemed to assuage some of Yani's concerns. Who could resist the perfect job appearing just when he only had a few months left of college? Bishop didn't think Yani could, and he knew Brandon was looking for a way to become active in the coalition after his own graduation. "Tell you what. I'll give you some small jobs over winter break. You four can test out the position first and then give me a formal answer this spring."

It was too good an opportunity to say no to. A no-strings-attached test drive plus a real job? He had them, hook, line, and sinker. Bishop wasn't surprised when Yani and Aaron both said yes together and were quickly echoed by Brandon and Luke.

Bishop nodded. "I will call you in a few days to set up the particulars. I know you all have work to catch up on for the classes you missed, so once the semester is over I'll have the first job lined up. Thank you."

Bishop stood and left the room. They would talk it over among themselves and the excitement would build. Bishop was happy for them and happy he could provide them with this opportunity, but mostly he was happy for the good they would do for the coalition. It was a cold stance to take, but it was also Bishop's job to take it. Later, he would slip into his role as Brandon's grandfather and be pleased with the benefits Brandon and his friends were getting, but for now he let the needs of the coalition be met first. It was the better option in the end, and he knew Yani, Aaron, Luke, and Brandon would eventually thank him for it.

At least he hoped so.

About Mell Eight

When Mell Eight was in high school, she discovered dragons. Beautiful, wondrous creatures that took her on epic adventures both to faraway lands and on journeys of the heart. Mell wanted to create dragons of her own, so she put pen to paper. Mell Eight is now known for her own soaring dragons, as well as for other wonderful characters dancing across the pages of her books. While she mostly writes paranormal or fantasy stories, she has been seen exploring the real world once or twice.

Facebook
www.facebook.com/MellEightFiction

Twitter
@MellEight

Website
www.melleightfiction.weebly.com

Other Books by Mell Eight

Ge-Mi: Part One
Ge-Mi: Part Two

Supernatural Consultant Series
Dragon Consultant
Dragon Deception
Dragon Dilemma
Dragon Detective
Dragon Soldier
Dragon Adventures
Dragon Lesson

Out of Underhill Series
Kelpie Blue

A Little Fairy Dust

Also from NineStar Press

Kelpie Blue by Mell Eight

When a beautiful blue horse asks Rin to go for a swim, Rin doesn't realize how much his life is about to change. Blue is unlike anyone else Rin has ever met, and the magic of the fae, and of this particular kelpie, is wondrous, but deadly. Rin learns too late he might be in for a swim he won't survive.

Dragon Consultant by Mell Eight

Dane, a supernatural consultant, is hired by the FAA to look into a series of reported dragon attacks on their planes. What Dane finds in the wooded area where the attacks took place is not quite the problem he expected: a group of dragon kits and their sick father hiding from the authorities.

When he learns the real reason the family was in the woods, his case grows more dangerous, and though Dane is experienced at both crime solving and watching his own back, taking care of baby dragons and their ill father makes everything else look easy.

A Little Faily Dust by Mell Eight

Nine tales of magic, love, and a little fairy dust: A military posting at the Rapunzel Tower to avoid war in *The Tower*; a Brownie that just wants to do something right in *Cleanly Wrong*; a dream of love unfulfilled in *A Heart's Dream*; saving the victims of an evil witch in *The Red Apple Witch*; a boy who just wants to go to the ball in *Cinder-Elle*; a cursed kingdom and search for lost love in *The Curse*; a thief and his fairy godparent with different ideas about love in *Happily Ever After*; a lightning strike, a lost egg, an ancient battle, and love at first spark in *Thunderbird*; and a prince trapped, knowing his true love will never save him in *The Beast*.

Connect with NineStar Press

Website: NineStarPress.com

Facebook: NineStarPress

Facebook Reader Group: NineStar Niche

Twitter: @ninestarpress

Instagram: NineStarPress

www.ingramcontent.com/pod-product-compliance
Lightning Source LLC
LaVergne TN
LVHW091542060526
838200LV00036B/670